Graffiti

Graffiti

PETRIE HARBOURI

BLOOMSBURY

For Nicholas Stavroulakis,
with love

First published 1998

Copyright © 1998 by Petrie Harbouri

The moral right of the author has been asserted

Bloomsbury Publishing plc, 38 Soho Square, London W1V 5DF

A CIP catalogue record for this book
is available from the British Library

10 9 8 7 6 5 4 3 2 1

ISBN 0 7475 3669 4

Typeset by Hewer Text Composition Services, Edinburgh
Printed in Great Britain by Clays Ltd, St Ives plc

CONTENTS

I

YOUR KARMA HAS RUN OVER MY DOGMA

Graffiti, London

When people meet and fall in love sparks fly. It is true, of course, that on the cosmic scale most of us are very small indeed, so that the sparks which we strike from each other's edges are insignificant to the point of being almost imperceptible – a kind of faint, briefly pulsing dust, soon to lose its evanescent glitter and be swept up casually with the rest of life's detritus. Sometimes, though, these sparks glow brighter, last longer. Sometimes from them is lit a hearth of enduring warmth and comfort. Occasionally – as legends tell us – they shake the world, set whole cities aflame, launch a thousand ships . . . And sometimes they merely sear and scorch, till hearts once tender are numbed with scar tissue.

It was only gradually that Tasos felt able to tell me about what had happened to him. At first his language was mundane: 'I met a girl,' he said. 'She wasn't anything special to look at, she was rather ordinary really, but I sort of fancied her.' Poor Tasos – it wasn't easy for him to find words with which to describe her. He wanted to say that her eyes changed colour with the changing light of day, that her thick glossy chestnut hair rippled faintly with each word she spoke, each breath she took, that her small breasts fitted perfectly into the palms of his hands. He wanted to say much more: to tell me how *alive* she was, how when he rested his head against her belly and heard the quiet regular murmurs of her body – the beating heart, the peristaltic gut, the secret filtering kidneys – he felt for the first time that he held in his hands an infinitely precious living animal. But all this was to emerge months later, expressed with great hesitation only after he started sleeping in my bed from time to time. At the beginning the best he could manage was, 'I fell in love with her,' then, very quietly, after a long pause, as if this statement was somehow inadequate, 'I *loved* her.'

So sparks flew. And the well-ordered fabric of Tasos's life began to shrivel and disintegrate in their heat. When he met Leonora Tasos had been married for close on sixteen years. He would probably have described himself as contented – though the subtext of this, communicated to me rather haltingly much later, was, 'I didn't know what was missing.' His life had fallen into an accepted and familiar pattern; the rhythms of existence were steady; domesticity, if occasionally a little stifling, was at any rate comfortable. And I suppose one shouldn't underestimate the importance of domestic comforts – before women went out to work and began to acquire some financial independence, the well-ironed shirts and the regular well-cooked meals were for a long time part of the wife's arsenal to prevent her husband straying too far from home . . . You could even say that mothers who brought their sons up to be dependent, incapable even of boiling an egg, formed the first link in this silken chain, this unconscious female conspiracy to keep their menfolk securely tethered. Neither Tasos nor his wife had ever given these matters much thought, yet I suspect she had a stronger sense of vested rights in Tasos than he had in her. The words 'my husband' have a different resonance from the words 'my wife'; 'my wife' only acquires an outraged possessive ring to it if it is the wife who is doing the straying. However, in this particular case Marianna remained a model of faithful wifehood and Tasos it was who fell in love.

I use the words 'fell in love' advisedly. For there are of course different kinds of adultery. If Tasos had indulged in the odd liaison with, for example, one of the girls at work, an occasional pleasant little *cinq à sept* conducted in some friend's bachelor apartment, ending with no hard feelings and perhaps some sentimental present, then Marianna (if she had known of it) might either have turned a histrionic blind eye with much heaving of theatrical sighs, or might have made a few ritual scenes ending in an equally theatrical forgiveness. I dare say she might even have felt a secret frisson of pleasure, compounded in equal parts of pride in the manliness of her husband and contempt for little-boy-men who can't keep their trousers zipped up but constantly need to prove themselves. And she might also have hugged to herself the knowledge that by thus transgressing her husband had played into her hands, altering the balance of power between them. The trouble was, though, that poor Tasos was innocent of all such transitory affairs and instead fell utterly in love with a slight green-eyed girl with crooked teeth and no breasts to speak of. Sex Marianna could have forgiven; love was outside the rules of the game.

I asked Tasos how his wife came to know of Leonora. 'I didn't tell her,' he answered, 'but she just seemed to know.' (In fact, as he was to discover, some kind friend had taken care to enlighten her.) If he had been slightly more experienced in extramarital affairs, Tasos might have been more discreet. As it was, he considered that discretion simply consisted of a lack of telephone calls and was unaware that his very obvious happiness and equally unmistakable lack of sexual interest in Marianna were colossal indiscretions. As someone a little wiser once pointed out to me, there are rules here too; pleading a headache is not solely a wife's prerogative and 'a hard day at work' is always a useful excuse which also serves to explain the occasional late return home. (I tend to steer clear of married men on the whole, since in my experience they're usually more trouble than they're worth, but once for a short space of time I was the third person in the triangle.) And if you are buoyantly, deliriously happy, he told me, the best thing to do is to put on a long face and say that you are worried about the state of the economy (in which your wife is sensibly not interested) or the children's education (in which she is extremely interested and about which she will hold forth at great length, leaving you free to savour the secret happiness in your heart). But of course all these time-honoured rules presuppose that you recognise the transitory nature of your affair and wish to preserve your home base intact.

As he began to speak more freely to me, Tasos explained that he had not really known what he wanted. Like all lovers he felt that Leonora was his destiny, that they were made for one another, that between them existed a bodily and spiritual communion which transcended all other ties, the only true, exquisite reality in his life. Yet when each evening he returned home and smoothly put his key into the familiar lock, opened the door, he entered into another solid and undeniable reality, so familiar that he could find his way round it in the dark. Leonora's flat was unpredictable, often untidy; she moved the furniture around, changed the pictures on the walls whenever the whim took her, she did not bother to wash the dishes if she was tired, her desk overflowed with papers and her bathroom with plants. Marianna's home was unchangingly immaculate, the good pieces of his parents' furniture carefully polished, the plants neatly ranged on the balcony, the bathroom spotless unless perhaps a lacy bra was hung out to drip neatly over the bath. (Ah, the mystique of the lace-clad female bosom: if you had asked Tasos in the past which bit of a woman he looked at first he would have answered 'her breasts', yet to his surprise Leonora's boyish figure moved him almost unbearably and when he had first slipped his hand under her T-shirt and established that *she didn't wear a bra* he had felt intense tenderness. Incidentally, if you had asked Marianna which bit of a man she looked at first I suspect she would have answered perfectly truthfully, 'his face', whereas Leonora apparently said, 'first his bottom, then his hands. I tend to judge a man's generosity of spirit by his bottom.' I must say I agree with this and always look at bottoms, though I generally cast a quick glance at the crotch first.)

But I am digressing. What all this amounted to was that Tasos was torn between two worlds – the karma of passion and the dogma of the status quo. Well, he isn't the first person to have found himself in this position and he certainly won't be the last. It's a painful position to be in, made worse by the conflicting threads of cultural and social expectations. On the one hand lies the romantic tradition: Tristan and Isolde, Romeo and Juliet, the world well lost for love. On the other hand lie all the worthy virtues of prudence and self-interest: security, stability, continuity, marriage, compromise. I suspect that most people find not too much difficulty in holding both these apparently contradictory views of life simultaneously, applying one in theory and the other, comfortably, in practice. For most of us are realistic enough to know that 'happily ever after' does not exist, that the great passions of our literature must be consummated in death before the lovers have time to grow old and grey and weary, that, failing a *liebestod*, passion may evaporate, love may stealthily and steadily turn to disenchantment, suppressed irritation and ever increasing anxious demands, ending perhaps in Emma's bottle of poison or the relentless wheels of Anna's train. For the world that was lost remains lost long after the love that justified everything has faded. Thus if we are honest we know that the best we can hope for is reasonable contentment, and strong social pressures discourage men and women from rocking the marital boat too violently.

Of course, if Tasos had possessed slightly more courage he might have jumped out of the boat altogether while there was still time, left Marianna, risked attempting to foster the sparks of love with Leonora into a steady flame of warmth and content. Retrospectively there is no way of knowing whether this could have worked. In any case, Tasos hesitated, agonised, was unable to come to any decision and ended up in a mess. He lost both Marianna and Leonora. He lost his familiar home after an acrimonious divorce in which Marianna salved her wounded vanity by pursuing him for everything he'd got. I never knew Leonora, for she left town before I met Tasos, so I have no idea what sort of love she felt for him; clearly, though, she was unable to bear the burden of his guilt and depression. Tasos himself admitted to me that he had thought of suicide. 'Whenever I took the train to work I used to stand at the edge of the platform and think of jumping. I didn't jump though. One day I saw the driver's eyes, and then I couldn't.' He half-smiled. 'I started going by bus instead, like you.' I kissed the palm of his hand without saying anything. (We were lying in bed peaceably after making love.) He paused. Over the couple of years that we have known each other he has come to feel comfortable enough with me to try to articulate his feelings. 'I think something had already died in me when Leonora left.'

I think he's right, and I think I know what had died in him: it was hope. This is one of the reasons that I have not suggested to Tasos that he move in with me. We meet several times a week and he generally stays here with me on Saturday nights. We get on well and I have become extremely fond of him; he's a gentle if not very passionate lover. I think he likes me too. But our present arrangement, living separately, seems to suit us both. Tasos already bears too many scars. And there are after all no sparks between us: I don't think either of us sees the other as his destiny – and anyway, I'm the wrong sex to fit into any conventional dogmatic view of things . . .

II

'WORDS, WORDS, WORDS'

Terrible things happen all around us every day. You only
have to turn on the television and watch the news to see
it: wars, bombings, floods, fires, famines, rapes, murders
– you name it, it will have happened somewhere today.
While you and I are picking at our dinner, having our third
glass of whisky, bedding our lover, someone somewhere is
screaming in agony. A lot of the time we'd rather not know.
But sometimes I can't help thinking that worse even than
indifference is our tendency to gloat, spectators of others'
misfortune and pain. The more terrible the road accident,
the more passers-by will have gathered round to have a
good look. If I were feeling charitable, I might perhaps say
that the mainspring of all this ghoulish voyeurism of horror
is some primitive need for Aristotelian catharsis, something
of a superstitious frisson along the lines of 'There but for the
grace of God go I'. I'm in a somewhat dyspeptic mood at
the moment, though, black spleen, and I can't say I think
much of God's grace. And while we're on the subject –
always assuming that we're talking of the Christian God –
have you ever paused to wonder what kind of sick religion
would choose as its central icon the image of a man tortured

to death? Have you ever stopped to imagine what crucifixion would really be like? Or worse, what sort of people could routinely hammer nails into someone's flesh, what sort of people would stand by and watch?

People like you and me, that's the answer. Yesterday I watched the children playing in the little park below my windows. I stood for about twenty minutes following their game as they darted to and fro in the thin spring sunlight, their energy apparently boundless, their voices as shrill as those of the swifts wheeling above them in the sky, and my stomach was twisted with terrible pity for them, infinite sadness for the imperfect and fallible cruelty of the lives that lay ahead of them. And – here's a sign of the times we live in – as I stood there one of the mothers came to collect her offspring, glanced up, saw me watching; her train of thought was quite clear from the sudden tensing of her facial muscles, from the way her movements became brisker, from the manner in which she caught hold of her child's arm and marched him off firmly as he called something to his friends over his shoulder: 'a paedophile' said her wary, protective mother's mind. She probably won't let her son play in this park again. And who am I to blame her? We all know of the dangers lying in wait for pink-cheeked, curly-haired, scruffy little boys. Though as it happens she couldn't have been more wrong, and my interests most certainly do not encompass children.

Yes, you're quite right: I'm depressed. And yes, I've been drinking a bit too much recently. I'm going easy on it this evening because of you. After all, if I ended up maudlin drunk or even worse lacrymose you'd probably leave pretty fast, wouldn't you? But I'm exaggerating: I don't usually drink myself silly, just enough to get to sleep.

Curious, isn't it, how it's often easier to speak openly and honestly with a total stranger than with one's nearest and dearest friends. Perhaps the problem with friends is that, no matter how much affection exists, we always want to present ourselves in the best light. Or maybe it's a matter of not wanting to burden our friends with the weight of our miseries; that sounds good and altruistic, doesn't it, but I suppose to be really honest I'd have to say that one doesn't want to risk *boring* them . . . Of course, it could quite simply be that I've only ever had one friend good enough to trust absolutely. Anyway, it makes one see the point of the confessional . . .

In my present black mood, though, I immediately start wondering if anyone ever speaks honestly about him or herself; for even in the confessional one might exaggerate one's sins, I suppose. Perhaps there is an innate human tendency to dramatise. You only have to listen to any conversation, no matter how banal, to see how trivial experiences, unimportant opinions, minor emotions, whatever, are exaggerated, how superlatives are debased: 'We had a *marvellous* time, it was simply *heavenly*' means 'We had a pleasant enough time and enjoyed ourselves', 'You are an absolute *angel*' means 'Thank you', and so on. The reverse side of this coin is the famous Anglo-Saxon understatement: 'Not bad', or the supremely colourless lower-middle class 'I don't mind if I do', meaning 'I very much want to . . .' ('fuck you like crazy', 'have another huge helping of your excellent Yorkshire pudding' or anything else where the timid English don't quite dare to express their appetite). In fact it's fascinating, isn't it, this English use of a double negative to make a scared little positive – on a par with some of their quaint old-fashioned euphemisms, like 'May

I show you the geography of the house?' meaning 'I'd better tell you where the lavatory is in case you want a pee.' (By the way, do you? It's the first door on the right down the passage and the light switch is outside.) Mind you, when it comes to euphemisms, the Americans really excel: do you know that in a recent translation of the Old Testament Saul is described as going into a cave in order to go to the bathroom? It's true, I promise you, I didn't make it up!

Yes, I agree, accuracy matters, although if one tries too scrupulously hard to be accurate there's always the risk that one may end up saying nothing at all. OK, there are silences and silences; there's the lovely companionable kind where nothing needs to be said, the hostile, biting, hurtful kind, or the really frightening silence of utter madness . . . Do you know *Othello*? I've always felt that the most shaking words are Iago's 'From this time forth I never will speak word' – a terrifying, chilly retreat don't you think, an utter denial of life. I suppose words are all that we have got with which to make some kind of sense of the things that happen to us.

That's what I've been doing, talking to you. Verbal therapy to get over a bit of heartbreak, not worth going into, the usual sort of story, you can probably guess. The sort of thing that leaves one feeling rather alone and scared of the brutality of life. I needed some company really: that's why I picked you up, I liked your face and I somehow didn't think I was risking brutality from you. (There, that's honest at least.) Actually I thought you looked lonely too.

Would you like to stay here tonight? Because you can sleep on the sofa if you want to, don't worry, I won't bother you. Only if you do want to stay can I just ask one thing? Please, Tasos, don't go away in the morning without saying goodbye, because for some reason that would really hurt.

III

Η ΕΥΤΥΧΙΑ ΕΙΝΑΙ Η ΑΓΝΟΙΑ ΤΗΣ ΔΥΣΤΥΧΙΑΣ

HAPPINESS IS THE
IGNORANCE OF UNHAPPINESS

Graffiti, Maroussi, Athens

The first time you realise that your husband is being unfaithful to you, your mouth goes dry. Your heart lurches, your stomach tightens uncomfortably as if gripped by a ghostly hand; the sun seems to go dark for a moment, the birds stop singing, everyday reality freezes. Of course after a few seconds things start flowing once more. Life goes on and you have to decide what to do about it.

Marianna had been half aware for some time of what the radiance emanating from Tasos implied. If asked, she would have asserted that they were happy together, that they got on well; this would not of course have been exactly true yet neither could it really be called a deliberate lie – quite simply it was what Marianna wished to believe. For it's only human, isn't it, to attempt to keep unpleasant things outside the periphery of your vision, to close your mind and avert your eyes from what you prefer not to see. Consciously Marianna thus refused to recognise that anything might be wrong; unconsciously she redoubled her efforts to please. (These efforts tended to involve long hours spent in the kitchen preparing elaborate dishes: Tasos, whose appetite seemed to have disappeared, noted the effort without understanding its causes and did not feel able to say, 'I'd really rather have just some salad and a bit of cheese.')

Unfortunately one's friends are sometimes determined to enlighten one. (Well-meaning? Malicious? Or just bored perhaps and getting a kick out of the drama of someone else's life?) And so one day Marianna's carefully willed edifice of ignorance was roughly demolished by a phone call: 'I think you really ought to know,' uttered with unctuous concern (a dreadful prologue this, almost as bad as 'If you don't mind me saying so . . .'). Then: 'She's about half his age' (an exaggeration), 'not particularly pretty, long hair, skinny little figure, nothing to write home about, but he seems *besotted*' (first subtext: 'Poor you, I do *so* sympathise, we all know what men are like don't we'; second subtext: 'What fun').

Let's take these subtexts one at a time. Marianna's friends – all of them Greek women secure in the comfortable certainties of their age and class – seemed to have some very definite ideas about what men, or at least husbands, were like. Some spoke of 'giving him a good talking to' or 'keeping him on a short rein' (husbands as naughty little boys? husbands as badly trained animals?), and one woman with a chronically errant spouse recommended putting up with his infidelity and indeed using it to gain the upper hand: 'All you have to do is make him feel the *tiniest* bit guilty, but not too much, don't overdo it, then he'll be so grateful you're not making a fuss that he'll be putty in your hands' (husbands as clay to be modelled). None of these women appears to have had any inkling that men might be something more than mere ciphers in the marital equation. Perhaps the truth is that few women have the faintest idea what men are like, and vice versa, which may be why genuinely warm friendship between the sexes is rarer than it should be – I mean so-called platonic friendships without a sexual component (and what a very strange use of poor Plato's name). Luckily, where a solid enough base of love and affection and esteem exists men and women are fairly skilled at using it to build personal bridges across this great divide. As for the second subtext, well, conceivably nothing is more amusing than the misfortunes of others, but for Marianna it was no fun at all.

When you discover for the first time that your husband is deceiving you, you have various options. The simplest (and often the wisest as long as his infidelity is of a fairly minor kind) is to do nothing, say nothing, grit your teeth. Of course you have to swallow down the outraged wail that rises within you: 'How could he do this to me?' Marianna's outrage stuck in her throat though, and swallowing was impossible. Indeed, outrage does not quite express her horrible, lurching sense of a blow to the very foundations of everything. Like so many of us, she had never given much thought to all the assumptions on which her life was based; thus she now found herself struggling with frightening new definitions, new equations. For there are some things that we imbibe in childhood and take so utterly for granted that we are at a loss if someone suddenly asks 'how do you know?' or 'why?': two and two is four, the square of the hypotenuse is equal to the sum of the squares of the other two sides, parallel lines meet at infinity . . . But what if it isn't so? What if parallel lives are doomed to run apart for ever, what if a new figure is factored into the well-known equation and the sums no longer add up, what if one and one equals happiness and you are not included? To change metaphors, what do you do if you suddenly realise that for years you've been making some very basic spelling mistakes? Marianna, it should be noted, had always subtly felt that she *owned* Tasos, whereas he *owed* her.

She would not have called herself a materialist, yet there is no doubt that possessions were of great importance to Marianna. This was not something she'd ever thought about very much of course, although once in a conversation with Tasos à propos of the drifting population of illegal, homeless, Albanian immigrants (whom she feared) she had said with surprising vehemence, 'It's not just that they're dirty and sleep rough in the park, it's that they don't *have* anything . . .' For possessions denote status, not only social status – though this too – but mainly *personal* status, and people without status do not fit into any recognisable scheme of things. It is indeed possible that Marianna unconsciously felt her own status to be slightly insecure because of her failure to produce children; at any rate, her small household gods of the domestic variety were a source of solace and affirmation, and marriage was intricately bound up with the ordered, comfortable, comforting possessions that went with it. She did not articulate it, could never have admitted it, but a husband constituted a sort of possession too, a very important if sometimes inconvenient one, his wedding ring a little bit similar to the collar and name-tag of a pet dog. Domestic animals, domestication, domesticity: but dogs may stray of course and husbands go tom-catting. And it is extremely frightening to see disorder, discomfort and dispossession loom threateningly on the horizon . . .

The insistent dull ache which Marianna felt at the very centre of her being was thus not any very straightforward kind of sexual jealousy. She did indeed accuse Tasos of 'screwing that little bitch' – yes, I know, people tend to use rather uncharacteristic language when they are angry –

but it was not the act itself that upset her; she felt that she might not have minded so very much if Tasos had been having a brief fling with some dumb blonde as she had at first half suspected, would really have faintly despised him: after all, it would have been 'only sex' (her words). It was rather the gossamer web of emotions surrounding this act that tormented her, or perhaps the simple fact that he desired someone else, excluded her, *was depriving her of her rights* even if she did not wish to exercise them so very often . . . Being excluded is miserable. It hurts.

Property, rights, debts: good legalistic words to use when one wants to shy away from love, warmth, tenderness, or for that matter from pain, hurt, misery. The debts were of course sexual. Poor Marianna: the strands of her feelings were interwoven in so complex a pattern here that it is rather hard to untangle them, but certainly among them was the notion, not 'I enjoy you and you enjoy me', but 'I offer my body for your enjoyment.' After she first confronted Tasos, an endless repetitive cycle of fruitless accusation and defence set in – she tense, he weary – yet neither of them managed to bring to the surface the years of suppressed lukewarm dissatisfaction. Thus Tasos ached with guilt without feeling able to justify himself, while Marianna remained stiff and icy instead of howling what she was really thinking at him with righteous indignation: 'I gave you my virginity' (a dubious gift, but like some heroine of a melodrama this was the way she saw it), or 'I never refused you anything' (in other words I'm a long-suffering saint and you're a brute). The first claim was literally true. The second less so, for there had been at least a couple of occasions on which Marianna had very definitely said no to Tasos; this she had conveniently forgotten, but even if she'd remembered she would have considered herself entirely justified – after all, surely there are proper norms in intercourse as in everything else . . . (I think at this point we should draw a decent veil and leave such matters where they belong, in the privacy of the bedroom; in case you are wondering, though, I might just note that what poor Tasos wanted was really not anything so very unusual.) In any case, debts are a sort of contract quite unenforceable if the debtor does not recognise himself as such. Their feelings had been at cross-purposes for so long that neither of them was now able to express to the other any essential painful truth.

It isn't hard for an outsider to see that even before Tasos fell in love their marriage had several weak points. Curiously, neither Tasos nor Marianna had recognised this. Or perhaps we shouldn't be surprised: another of those business-like words which could be applied is 'investment'. And of course it's only human not to want to admit to yourself that the company in which you have invested your entire fortune is going bust. Thus both of them might have continued for years – to the end of their lives perhaps – without ever acknowledging the essential unhappiness that lay beneath the surface of their conventional, placid existence. Tasos was in the end forced to acknowledge it. Marianna never did. To admit that their serene and apparently contented life together had perhaps been nothing more than the thinnest of veneers over solitude and emptiness was impossible for her. Souls can be fed the wrong diets just as bodies can; long starved but ever unable to reach out and pluck the sun-warmed golden fruit from the tree of life, Marianna drew what meagre sustenance she could from the cheap junk food of anger, revenge and injured innocence.

When you feel threatened you fight as best you can . . . Marianna thus hit out at Tasos with every last ounce of her not inconsiderable energy, determined to wound. She was quite perceptive enough to be aware of his tender, vulnerable points. With the unerring precision of an accomplished surgeon she applied her probes where they would hurt most, employed her scalpels – sterilised with icy contempt – to excise, without anaesthetic, the maximum amount of living tissue . . . Neutered tom-cats are clean animals who stay at home: and the operation she had set out to perform was effectively one of emasculation, a kind of long, slow castration.

When genies grant us our wishes, though, we often find that there's a hidden catch, that they are not quite what we really wanted. By then it is too late to turn back. So it was with Marianna. During the last few hateful weeks of their life together she was frequently appalled by the sound of her own voice, wished she could unsay some of the wounding words, longed to stretch out her hand, to stroke his hair and say 'I'm sorry' . . . But once the basic assumptions of a marriage are gone, nothing more you can do has any effect and your tentative advances are merely met with weary distaste by a victim who no longer cares. When all that remains is a bleak wasteland of pain too awful to contemplate it's best to remove your gaze from it. Thus, sore and bruised, Tasos finally moved out and Marianna, miserable, consulted the best lawyer she could find.

IV

GENGHIS KHAN, TASOS CAN'T

Graffiti, London (modified)

'Wasn't it a rather odd career move to ask to be transferred here?'

'Oh, I felt like a change, anyway provincial towns have their advantages, maybe I wasn't really suited to all the back-stabbing and competition of the city.'

'In any case, I am extraordinarily glad that you did.' He smiled at her.

'Actually,' she said some time later, lighting a cigarette for him, 'it wasn't really a reasoned decision, more of a moment of panic, a wild leap, a desperate urge to run away . . .'

'What from?'

'The usual.'

'A love affair?'

'Yes.'

'So I had imagined. But what made you run?'

. . . A love affair, a love affair, she mused. I didn't think it was an affair, I thought it was love. Well, in fact I didn't really *think* anything, I just felt: I felt we belonged together, I felt we fitted like the two halves of a shell, enclosing a secret, wordless, quivering universe of rightness. After the beginning – when we talked endlessly, delightedly, words upon words, phrases on phrases, sentences, implications, our minds as eager to intertwine as our bodies – yes, after the beginning there were often times when we barely spoke. We'd lie in bed and laugh out loud, not at anything, just from happiness; as dusk fell we wouldn't bother to put on the light but would lie there companionably, scarcely able to make out each other's smile in the half-dark, yet each knowing, *apprehending*, the other's smile with every atom of our being. And I ran away . . .

'Why did I run? Oh, I don't know, cowardice I suppose, weakness: as soon as things got complicated I somehow couldn't cope. Not very admirable, was it?'

She turned towards him, smiling tentatively, pleading, seeking reassurance.

'Why did it get complicated?'

'Oh,' vaguely, 'you know . . .'

'Married, was he?'

'Yes, of course, but that was hardly *my* fault' (with some asperity).

'All right, calm down, I wasn't criticising. Poor love, was he just playing around with you then?'

'No, it wasn't like that, I don't think he was playing, he simply didn't really know what he wanted.'

. . . He wanted *me*, he wanted *me*, he wanted *me*. I didn't trust my own judgment: always a mistake. All those stereotypes: the philandering husband looking out for an easy lay, having a bit on the side (ah, how I hate those revolting expressions), but always returning to the lawful wedded wife, securely entrenched in her wedding-ringed position, mother of his children (thank God, at least, that he didn't have any), washer of his underpants, provider of his favourite meals, nurse of his minor ailments, claiming him nightly in the marital bed . . . And then the 'other woman': the predatory, irresponsible siren, luring him into temptation, unsanctioned by society, always the loser in the end. God, what rubbish. Things aren't so simple. The trouble is, though, that it's more comfortable for people to think that they are; we all like putting things into pigeonholes, even – perhaps especially – other people's relationships. Or perhaps things often really are like this, perhaps like every mistress I'm deluding myself, wanting to believe that in our case it was different . . .

It *was* different though: I've never doubted that he loved me. Where I went wrong was in listening to all the sane, commonsense voices of friends – 'He'll never leave his wife' – instead of having the courage of my convictions. Deep inside I never really thought of myself as a 'mistress' (lovely, stately, old-fashioned word) or as 'the other woman'; I was myself and he was himself and we smiled at each other and our bodies met in exquisite harmony and we were happy. It is true that in all our time we only ever spent one whole night together, that there were moments when I sat by the telephone willing it to ring, that I was always aware of his other life, always familiar with the shiver of slipping my hand into his trouser pocket and feeling the solid metal of the key that unlocked the door into his other existence. Casual, meaningless, insignificant objects can be impregnated with meaning: all his small personal possessions were touched with magic and beauty: his keys, his wallet, his watch, his driving licence, his pen, even his loose change.

All of them accompanied him throughout the day, were with him when I was not, nestling close in his pockets against the warmth of his body. Sometimes I used to touch them surreptitiously, wishing him all unbeknown to his wife to carry some lingering caress of my fingers into his everyday life. Once I happened to see him and his wife together at the theatre. He didn't see me (my friends and I were in cheaper seats). She was younger and better looking than I had imagined her to be (I know: wishful thinking), with a low-cut black dress revealing her curvaceous bosom. They didn't seem to have very much to say to one another . . .

Where he went wrong was in being afraid of her. I dare say he couldn't help it. At the beginning we did not stop to think of consequences; we assumed in some way that we'd be together without bothering to work out the dreary logistics of it all. And by the time we might have begun to do so it was already too late: some malicious and supposedly well-meaning friend had told her about me ('Tasos is seeing some girl, you'd better step in before it goes any further'). She turned the full battery of her heavy artillery on him and flattened him. I've never told anyone quite what happened during those last weeks, but the truth is that he became completely impotent. Of course I told him that it didn't matter, that we could be patient, etc., etc., but equally of course it did matter. Apart from anything else, it demolished the last shreds of his already tenuous self-confidence. He hesitated in anguished indecision and I turned on him, I savaged him. And I ran away. I can't help thinking that if perhaps we'd had more time, so that he could have found the certainty and the courage to come to a decision, to tell his wife himself, so that I could have learnt more wisdom, then we might possibly have had a chance . . .

Of course, the brutal truth is that we *did* have a chance, we had the sort of chance that is only given to you once in a lifetime, we held the mysterious and priceless essence of love in our cupped hands – but our hands were weak and frail, our fingers opened, and it slipped away for ever . . .

I have naturally wondered sometimes whether two such cowards as ourselves would have been happier if we'd never met. I used to think at any rate that for Tasos things might have been better if the even tenor of his life had run on undisturbed. A couple of months ago, though, when I went back home to visit my family, I ran into an old friend (yes, another of those interfering busybodies) who told me something rather strange about Tasos. He is apparently now living quite openly with a young man. It upset me a lot at first. But a few days later this man was pointed out to me in a café; I sat and watched him for a long time, as discreetly as I could, and I have to say that I liked his face – for it seemed to be intelligent and kind. My friend said, 'There, you're well rid of him, you had a lucky escape.' I don't see it quite like this: I think Tasos has found a refuge, I'm glad that he has and I hope it lasts . . .

She smiled.

'What are you thinking?' he asked.

'Oh, about life and love and second chances,' she replied.

She shook the hair back from her face. 'I'm hungry,' she said. 'Shall we get dressed and go and find something to eat?'

'Good idea.' He hugged her and got up.

. . . I know there are never any second chances, but I can't help hoping that Tasos has by some miracle been offered one. I know there are no second chances, which is why I am not saying any of this aloud, but I am in need of the warmth that you offer and so one day before too long I may well agree to marry you.

V

ΠΛΑΣΤΟΙ ΑΝΘΡΩΠΟΙ ΠΛΑΣΤΕΣ ΑΝΑΓΚΕΣ

FAKE PEOPLE, FAKE NEEDS

Graffiti, Maroussi, Athens

'I have a deep psychic need for you,' someone once said, and 'Rubbish,' was my reply. I don't much believe in deep psychic needs – except of course for those that we all share: for love and warmth, for a place that feels like home. The kind that people speak too much of I invariably suspect to be fake. I told Felix this one day. He laughed. 'Sometimes,' he said, 'I look in the mirror and it occurs to me . . .' But at that point the doorbell rang, then Felix himself had to leave, running down the stairs two at a time, so I never discovered what he had been going to say or what it had to do with fakes. Much later, however, he said of Fanny, 'She's not really eccentric at all, it's just that she's the only person one's ever met who never pretends or fakes anything.' He added, 'A bit disconcerting at first, but awfully comfortable in the end, don't you think?'

There are strangely uncomfortable moments in city life when you are overcome by a feeling of deep unease. It has something of loneliness in it, though 'apartness' might be a better word; for it is in a minor rather than a major key, not so much a feeling of desperate isolation as the sense that you are cut off from your surroundings, that everything going on around you suddenly bears no relation whatsoever to yourself. The voices of children playing in the square, the grinding groundswell of traffic, punctuated by horns honking, brakes squealing, the music blaring from the neon-lit kebab shop on the corner: all of them for an instant become so alien that your ears and brain suspend them, they fade into an indistinct dull background murmur, and all that remains in the foreground is the rasping of the day's last cicadas in the pollarded mulberry tree, the hooting of the evening's first owls, the beating of your own heart. This at least was Felix's experience.

Felix always needed a sense of space. It was for this reason that he had decided to sit in the rather humble little square until the tail-end of the rush hour had abated, rather than fight his way on to an overcrowded bus and travel wedged in among other people's tired and not so recently washed bodies. Perhaps his moment of urban angst – that brief, abrupt divorce from the life around him – was unconsciously triggered by the graffiti on the wall of the barracks opposite him, where the foot-high black letters of someone's spray-can proclaimed like an accusation, 'fake people, fake needs'. Felix's own conclusion was, 'I probably need a drink'; all the same he made no move to get up, continued to sit in the twilight, to wait and to listen. And met Fanny.

'I was listening to the owls,' he said severely when – much later – I asked him where he and Fanny first met. 'It was a classic pick-up. She fixed her beady eyes on me as I sat there innocently minding my own business, sidled over and started chatting me up.'

'I was intrigued by the rapt expression on his face,' explained Fanny.

Felix did not much like this word; Fanny had been amused by 'sidled' and was perhaps having her gentle revenge.

'I was not in the least rapt,' he said. 'I was merely trying to listen to Athena's owls.'

Neither Fanny's age nor her figure permitted sidling; in truth she had simply walked up to the bench and sat down, firmly and confidently. Then, aware of his slight tensing, of the way he edged imperceptibly towards his own end of the bench, of the fixity with which his gaze suddenly focused on the dusty palm tree behind the graffiti wall, with its shaggy collar of dead fronds, she had looked at him and spoken: 'Do you mind if I sit here for a bit?'

Had it been someone else Felix might have been honest, might have said, 'Yes, I mind, I wanted to be alone'; the fact that she was an elderly woman inhibited him, however, so that he resorted instead to the automatic polite formula of, 'No, of course not, please . . .' and thereby scored bad marks. I don't think one can really blame him – I would probably have done the same, and you would too perhaps. After all, there is a sort of etiquette which Fanny had infringed, an unwritten code of practice for sitting on park benches that are already occupied. Whether or not you sit down at all will be regulated by age and sex (your own, the occupant's), and questions such as how close you sit, where you direct your gaze and so on are governed by a subtle set of rules that in turn depend on what hopes, expectations, invitations or lack of them you wish to signal. Unless they have something specific in mind, co-occupants of park benches rarely speak to each other. Fanny though had always had a code of her own.

'Young man, I rather suspect you may be a bit of a liar,' she said.

This was unexpected. Felix turned and faced her.

'Of course I'm a liar sometimes,' he answered. 'I dare say you are too.'

The tone of this response, dispassionate, neither defiant nor defensive, scored very high marks indeed in Fanny's reckoning.

'Well, that was honest at least,' she said.

'Perhaps now is the moment to say something about all Cretans being liars,' he said.

'Oh, I think we can take that as read.'

Each watched the other for a moment, then both laughed.

On the whole I tend to think that people who are going to find themselves in sympathy with one another usually know it within seconds. For Felix and Fanny at any rate this was so, and within a very short time they were having the first of many drinks together, sitting at her kitchen table and looking out over the cemetery, black now save for the occasional flicker of tiny oil lamps on some graves. 'You always pay a lower rent for flats that overlook cemeteries,' Fanny explained. 'People are frightened at being so near the dead, you see, superstitious and uncomfortable at the reminder that there's a point beyond which nothing can be faked.' Noticing that Felix's own expression was faintly uncomfortable, she said, 'Actually I like it. I like the greenness of it by day, the darkness of it by night, the big trees. The dead are peaceful neighbours. And for you who like owls it's a good place,' she added, 'a whole colony of them seem to live there.' (It has always rather pleased me,' Felix had said, 'that for the last two and a half thousand years or so the Greek equivalent of "coals to Newcastle" has been "owls to Athens".' Then, in a sudden moment of confidence, 'I dream of owls sometimes. The best dream I ever had was of holding a perfect, vulnerable, trembling silvery-brown owl in my hands and knowing from its eyes that it understood I wouldn't hurt it.')

'Fanny is a witch,' Joshua was later to pronounce. 'She looks at you over her spectacles and obliges you to confess your most shaming secrets.' Felix disagreed: 'She doesn't oblige you and she's not a witch, she just makes you feel you *can* confess.' Perhaps Joshua and Felix both felt the need for a confessor from time to time (and if so, then there was surely nothing fake about this need) or perhaps Fanny did indeed possess some quality that encouraged people to tell her things – maybe it is simply that for a lot of people plumpness equals motherliness. However this may be, the fact is that within an hour of meeting her Felix had confessed to Fanny one of his two most private secrets. Joshua incidentally was also aware of it (indeed, although he did his best to conceal it, it would be hard to know Felix for any length of time without noticing this fact about him); however, it is only fair to Joshua to say that it was something about which he had always scrupulously refrained from teasing Felix. Quite why Felix was so terribly ashamed of this particular secret is unfathomable. Nevertheless Fanny extracted it relatively painlessly . . . In the entrance hall of her building she pressed the button for the lift (having suggested that a drink in her kitchen would be more comfortable than a conversation on a park bench), and Felix said as casually as possible, 'I'll walk up. Which floor?'

'It's all right,' she said, 'the lift may be old but you're slender and it can perfectly well manage both of us.'

'I'd prefer the stairs, truly, it's good exercise,' he insisted.

Fanny appeared to accept this. 'Fifth floor then.'

As they sat drinking though, having talked of graveyards and owls and dreams, she suddenly asked, 'Do you really need the exercise, Felix?'

He didn't pretend not to understand what she was referring to. 'Yes, indeed I do, of course I do, I lead a fearfully sedentary life.'

A pause. Fanny smiled gently, said nothing. Felix swallowed.

'Actually, the truth is that I'm just not terribly fond of lifts.' The confession was made. 'I don't awfully like horrid little enclosed spaces.' Then, slightly defensively, 'I use them if I absolutely have to, you know, the 30th floor or something. I shut my eyes and take a deep breath and repeat a childish prayer.'

'What about other things? Cars, buses?'

'Cars aren't a problem. Buses are all right if they're not too crowded and I can sit or stand by a window.'

'And aeroplanes?'

'Oh God, perfectly dire. I manage by doping myself silly. Please don't laugh.'

She didn't, and moreover never mentioned the subject again.

The secret that Felix was most sensitive about, however, had to do with his name. Naming a child is a great responsibility, and we all know of cases where social aspirations, misplaced romanticism or family piety have led parents to saddle their children with the most terrible names, which must then be borne like a life sentence. Some people seem to suffer from the simple inability to *hear* the sound of a name or *see* the shape that its letters make on paper. Our name defines us perhaps: Roy and Rex may turn out very different from

Ephraim or Epaminondas. And thus occasionally it happens that a name – however inoffensive it may appear – causes its bearer enduring misery since it feels wrong, incompatible with his or her true identity. This was Felix's case. On the whole he avoided speaking of the subject, though once at a dinner party he referred to the problem – in one of his more pretentious (and unguarded) moments – as 'onomastic dysphoria'; he refrained, of course, from mentioning that he himself had managed to wriggle free of his own given name (his private image for this was 'like a snake sloughing off an old and constricting skin'), and soon deftly steered the conversation on to gender dysphoria – transsexuals being a subject which people at dinner tables seem unable to resist. Fanny's name, though, also presented problems for Felix.

'Oh dear,' he said at their second meeting, 'Fanny is an awfully *rude* name to give to someone, I really don't think I can call you Fanny, I'll just have to stick with a non-committal "you" until I come up with something more suitable.'

'Very well. Yours, at any rate, is a good name.'

'Yes, isn't it.' And then to his surprise Felix heard himself saying, 'I chose it myself actually, it just seemed to suit,' and went miserably pink at the unwonted admission. Fanny noticed the blush and did not ask, whereupon Felix felt able to say, 'I was christened Francis.'

'Well, dear boy, it could have been worse. Makes us namesakes in fact. Fanny is short for what I was christened, which was Francine.'

They both laughed.

'If I promise never to divulge Francine, will you swear to keep quiet about Francis?'

'Yes, Felix,' she said, and kept her word.

The neighbourhood where Fanny lives is gradually becoming smart. She worries that her rent may soon go up dramatically, though when I tried delicately to hint that perhaps I could help with it she told me that Felix had already offered but that so far she could manage. The mulberry tree is still there, though the square has been repaved and replanted as part of a pedestrian area. The cemetery is much the same as it always was, though increasingly running out of space for its occupants; the dead are not permitted to rest in peace for more than five years before being exhumed (their weary bones are then bundled up and placed in an ossuary). Felix says how dreadful to be overcrowded even after death, and wishes the Orthodox Church would allow cremation. He claims there are fewer owls these days. The ochre buildings of the old barracks have been restored and transmogrified into a cultural centre; the palm tree has been shorn of its accumulated weight of dead fronds and the old graffiti cleaned off the wall (needless to say, new graffiti appeared overnight, unfortunately of a less interesting variety).

I was having problems again with my 'deep psychic need' man and was wondering how to extricate myself.

'When it comes to needs,' said Fanny firmly, 'I do believe there are only two kinds – real ones and false ones.'

'Darling Deborah,' said Felix, 'there's something I've always meant to ask – was it you who wrote that old graffiti about fake needs?'

She laughed. 'No, it wasn't me . . . I might have done, I suppose, but I never thought of it. Anyway, someone else got in first.'

I too was curious: 'Felix, why do you call Fanny "Deborah"?'

'Oh,' he replied, 'that's very simple. It's because she is the justest of judges, that's mainly why, but it's also a bit to do with the place she lives, the barracks and the palm tree.'

Fanny chuckled. 'One of the reasons I love this boy is that he's the only person I know who can make Old Testament puns.'

'Ah well,' said Felix happily, 'that's what comes of being brought up in a bible-reading family.'

My own agnostic education had left some gaping lacunae, so that I could not pick up the allusion. I spent hours the following evening thumbing through a borrowed bible and finally found the reference: Judges 4, 4–6.

VI

'MENE MENE TEKEL UPHARSIN'
'... THOU ART WEIGHED IN
THE BALANCES AND ART
FOUND WANTING ...'

(Daniel 5, 25–7)

How odd of God to choose to communicate in graffiti. There can be something rather sinister about a message written on a wall, can't there? It generally appears mysteriously overnight: one day nothing, then suddenly as you go by on your way to work the next morning there it is ... And while graffiti of political or sexual content are usually fairly predictable, the other kind – the cryptic kind – are the ones that you puzzle over, that you apply to yourself or not as the case may be, that sometimes you find surprisingly grim. God's message to Belshazzar was one of the grimmest. 'The writing was on the wall,' we say (well, if we like speaking in clichés we say it), yet we forget – if we ever knew – quite what this writing meant. *Tekel*: you have been weighed in the balances and been found wanting: a terrible judgment.

It's not a verdict we'd want to have to apply to ourselves. Though of course if we were judged according to our just deserts we'd probably all be found wanting. It's a good thing that on the whole people temper their self-judgment with a liberal dose of mercy and thus generally manage to muddle along through life comfortably enough. If a few of your acquaintances find you wanting from time to time, this does no great harm. But if the entire web of your life frays and disintegrates beyond repair so that you start weighing *yourself* in the balances, then what? The judgment is terrible, you lose your courage: that's the briefest answer.

This is more or less what had happened to Tasos. On the April night that he first met Felix his courage had been at a very low ebb indeed. There is something about evenings in springtime that makes it doubly hard to be on your own. Perhaps it is a primitive recognition of the resurgence of nature to which we are still attuned, even if we are not consciously aware of it – for even in the heart of the city the evidence of life's renewal is perceptible all around us in the tender green of new leaves. After the sun sets it is chilly, yet the winter mood is gone, people's movements are freer and more expansive as they walk along the streets. There is hope in the air. But if in your heart there is hopelessness, then April is indeed the cruellest of months. Tasos generally passed his evenings alone at home (if home is the right word to describe the small furnished flat he had moved into after leaving his wife), yet on this particular night some springtime restlessness made him go out. Unlike Felix, he was not in the habit of translating his feelings into thoughts; thus it was with the inarticulate longing of the dumb beast to seek the warm, reassuring comfort of the herd that he made his way to the most crowded café he could find. And there he sat, quiet and still and anonymous, bathed in the cheerful wash of other people's noise. And there Felix found him.

'You stood there and said, "*Do you mind if I join you for a bit?*" and I was about to say, "*Please leave me alone,*" but I looked up and you were blushing as if you'd had second thoughts, yet you stood your ground, you had a sort of dignity that made me not want to reject you.' Thus this improbable meeting. Felix always believed that it was some providential angel who steered their paths through space and time till they met at this particular moment – but then Felix had his own way of seeing things and was indeed more than a little superstitious (in his pocket he carried a small silvery fragment of sea-washed wood, found long ago on a beach, so that he could always touch it when the need arose for apotropaic magic; he was a great believer in not tempting providence and, had he lived a couple of generations earlier, would have prefaced all his minor plans for the following day or week with a 'Deo volente'). Tasos – rationalist – simply felt that it was chance.

The plain truth, of course, is that both wanted company. And 'want' is a very strong little word, isn't it, carrying a whole range of partly overlapping and partly complementary meanings: desire, need, lack . . . Perhaps this reflects some truth about human feelings: either we are too muddled to tell the difference between these meanings or – a more ordered view – we need what we lack and desire what we need. In any case, on that particular April evening hope and despair and loneliness and want combined to propel Tasos and Felix towards some kind of friendship. For if things had been slightly different (if the one had not been unable to face the thought of going home alone or the other had not been floundering in the kind of despair that comes from being found wanting), then their rather disparate needs and lacks would not have met in the shared desire for a little simple human warmth.

I'm speaking of the very simplest kind of warmth: the mere presence of another person who has no preconceptions about you, makes no assumptions, no demands. You don't need me to tell you that there's another fairly simple kind –

36

sex – which at first sight might have seemed like a foregone conclusion to what was after all effectively a pick-up. Things don't necessarily follow the most probable paths, though. Felix always says that you can *smell* if the other person is sexually interested in you: 'I knew perfectly well that Tasos was not interested, and I also knew that he knew that I knew.' Subliminal messages were thus passed to and fro between them, with the result that neither felt the need to discuss the matter and both felt somehow comforted and eased by the sense of communication. After the café closed they went back together to Felix's flat and sat talking for another hour or so. Neither spoke very much of himself. Both, however, were remarkably more relaxed than at the beginning of the evening.

Now, if we are thinking in terms of probabilities, the most likely outcome of this chance encounter one spring evening would have been – precisely nothing. Each would have retreated once more into his shell, with a sense perhaps of having ventured too far, having acted indiscreetly out of character; Tasos would have thanked Felix politely for his hospitality, they would have gone their separate ways and by summer would more or less have forgotten each other. It didn't happen quite this way though. It's true that Tasos was polite, and it's certainly true that they made no arrangements to meet again, yet during the weeks that followed each thought rather a lot about the other. When your morale is low, your confidence in yourself shaken and your courage almost drained away it helps no end to think about someone else; Felix wondered, 'Is he managing OK?' and Tasos thought, 'I hope he's all right,' and for both a faint flicker of light briefly glowed.

Felix in fact dreamed of Tasos a couple of times, fairly

simple wish fulfilment dreams that I see no need to describe in detail. Tasos did not dream of Felix. Nevertheless, a few weeks later it was Tasos who picked up the telephone one Saturday afternoon and invited Felix to have dinner with him. This second meeting very nearly got off to a bad start. Felix hesitated, anxiety and doubt flowed over Tasos:

'I suppose it's rather short notice, never mind, sorry, I'll call you another time perhaps . . .'

'No, wait, I'd like it, I'd love to have dinner with you, Tasos, just tell me where and what time.'

And the rendezvous was fixed. When they met, matters were not much better. Neither was quite at ease; the atmosphere was one of slightly self-conscious constraint. 'Oh hell,' thought Felix, and 'After all, I was wrong, I should have left it, we're strangers,' thought Tasos.

Saturday night is a busy time for restaurants. Luckily, as it turned out. For the restaurant where Tasos had intended taking Felix was full and thus they ended up eating at a much humbler taverna round the corner.

'I'm sorry, I should have thought to make a reservation,' apologised Tasos.

'Actually I like this better,' said Felix, suddenly beginning to feel comfortable again. 'Anyway, I'm not wearing a tie, and it *was* rather a tie sort of place wasn't it, a tie-you-down sort of place, and a place so full of reservations that I'd probably have been far too reserved to say anything and you would have had to eat your dinner in a resounding silence.'

'I doubt that, you know, Felix.'

'You think I talk too much?' (sub-flirtatious smile).

'I like to hear you talk' (perfectly serious smile).

The atmosphere was once more easy.

★　　★　　★

I don't know what weights Jehovah put into the scales when he found Belshazzar so gravely wanting. I know, though, that when people find themselves or each other wanting the weights are reproaches, demands, failures . . . And one of the reasons for all the petty failures is the sort of self-pride that prevents us from being direct and honest. Felix's initial hesitation on the telephone had of course been due to the common kind of pride that makes us wish to camouflage our feelings and appear offhand. (To say nakedly that we've been sitting by the phone waiting for it to ring makes us seem too *hungry*, too dependent; we don't like admitting need and prefer to seem thoroughly well fed and fully clothed in self-sufficiency.) Each time we succumb such pride weighs against us in the scales. Demands (the heaviest of weights) in turn tend to arise from expectations, from definitions of what the other person should be. Happily Felix overcame his pride, while Tasos had presumably jettisoned his from the moment that he picked up the phone. Neither could envisage any very clear definition of their relations. The conventions of defensiveness were thus suspended for a while; they relaxed their guard, were content to accept each other without judgment, mutually offering a much needed companionable warmth with the scales evenly balanced. For once there was no writing on the wall.

VII

'I COULD BE BOUNDED IN A NUTSHELL AND COUNT MYSELF A KING OF INFINITE SPACE WERE IT NOT THAT I HAVE BAD DREAMS'

The first thing that attracted me about Tasos was his smell. I had noticed him at once (for I always cast an eye round to see whatever is to be seen) and I'd briefly thought how sad he looked, but I was talking to some people that I knew and thus didn't pay much attention. After they left, though, I didn't feel like going home, decided to allow myself one more drink. Better have a pee first, I thought. And it was as I was making my way back that I passed close to Tasos and caught a faint whiff of him. It was a *lovely* smell, fresh and green and sweet, something like the smell of new-mown grass in springtime. He was sitting by himself, both his hands clasped round what looked like an empty glass, his manner quiet, his mind clearly elsewhere. Smells are so evocative, aren't they, awakening such bittersweet nostalgia for youth and innocence, the wisteria on sunny walls in some far distant world, the jasmine and honeysuckle of courtyards irretrievably gone, paradises long since lost . . . Don't laugh, but in that noisy, crowded café with its end-of-evening atmosphere compounded of smoke and liquor and the cheap perfumes of women Tasos smelt pure and clean. I spoke without pausing for thought: 'May I join you for a little while?' He looked up. (Jesus Christ, are you out of your mind, it's the wrong sort of place, he's the wrong sort of person . . .) For a moment he said nothing, then, rather gravely, 'Sit down.' And then he smiled at me, not a come hither sort of smile, I don't mean that, just a brief, friendly, *human* sort of smile.

I was right and Tasos *was* sad that evening. He's a rather private person though, and certainly not a very verbal one, so he told me little about himself then except that he had recently been divorced. I had already deduced this, having observed the pale mark on his finger where until lately a broad gold wedding ring had been. And here's a fascinating question: at what point do you take the ring off – when you first separate, when the divorce becomes final, or when? And what do you do with it – throw it away, melt it down? Or if you've been married several times do you keep a little hoard of wedding rings? I suppose everyone has his own way of dealing with the tokens and symbols, the unhappy, empty little remains left on the shore after the tide has gone out. (Myself, I buried them furtively one evening under a tree in the park, and then went home and had a good cry.) Anyway, the question remains unanswered because I didn't ask. Tasos came home with me that night as if it was the most natural thing in the world and slept on my sofa as if we were old familiar friends. I liked having him there. I liked *him* in fact: his smile, his rather pleasant voice, his beautiful smell.

Everybody has his or her own smell, you know. This has got nothing to do with washing or not washing, it's just an essential, utterly individual part of us, a sort of olfactory equivalent to fingerprints. And thank God we still possess the primitive ability to detect and to respond to these scents. It occurs to me that when people speak rather tritely about 'the chemistry being right' between lovers, perhaps what they really mean is that each likes the other's scent . . . After all, you'd be most unlikely, wouldn't you, to leap into bed with someone whose smell you didn't like, and if you did so by mistake (too drunk to perceive it, too desperate to care), then you'd probably leap out again pretty fast before too long. I have to admit it makes me feel a tiny bit queasy to imagine the engulfing female effluvium of an unwashed Josephine, yet – always supposing that he liked that kind of thing – I can perfectly well understand Napoleon. Incidentally, thinking of washing, one of the rather happy side effects of the late-twentieth-century angst about natural products, dangerous chemicals, allergies and so forth is that it is now quite easy to buy the unperfumed soaps and shampoos that I have always preferred.

'I like the contrast between your bathroom and you,' Tasos told me over breakfast that first morning. He had been drinking his coffee rather quietly. I sensed a quality of withdrawal in the atmosphere, of uncertainty, of ambivalences – not the obvious ones, yet perceptibly something – that I was not well enough attuned to him to understand. Nevertheless, one of his brief, expressive smiles accompanied this statement. I asked him to explain. He paused to find the words he wanted, then came up with: 'You are a very colourful person, I think, and your bathroom is quite startlingly white.' He's right about the last bit; as well as hating perfumed deodorants and so on, I also particularly loathe rose pink or baby blue baths and basins or – even more dire – avocado green . . . After he left, though, I worried a bit about 'colourful': did he mean that I was a trifle too much glorious Technicolor for his taste? I have two comforting little mantras which I repeat to myself from time to time; one is, 'I am that I am,' and the other Pope's, 'Whatever is, is right.' That day was a Pope day. There is also a third mantra, an everyday composite one: 'It doesn't matter, never mind, it'll all come out in the wash.'

But presumably it is likely to be some time before the great cosmic Launderer gets to work. So I lay down on the sofa where Tasos had spent the night, burying my face in the cushions, breathing in his lingering green and golden scent (sunshine, birdsong, fresh-mown hay), thinking about bathrooms . . . It's a fact that in most modern apartments the bathrooms are definitely mean and narrow. They may be lavishly appointed, all tiles and gleaming taps and what have you, yet the people who design such buildings work hard to save space and 'living rooms' are extended as much as possible at the expense of everything else. Odd, really: the most important bits of *my* living take place in the bedroom and the kitchen and the bathroom . . . But according to the received middle-class wisdom the public spaces – for show – are given priority over the private spaces. That's why, when I finally managed to get a place of my own, I didn't bother even looking at modern buildings but searched till I found this flat on the third floor (top floor, no lift) of a once grand, now faded old building. The crumbling stucco outside doesn't bother me; I like its high ceilings and long passages. And yes, I love my bathroom, it is spacious and gleaming white, functional and uncluttered; I take refuge there sometimes, and lie in a warm bath listening to Bach. I usually have a vase of flowers on the shelf above the basin: my favourites are yellow roses. And I have a strange and rather comfortable low wooden chair to sit on that I picked up in a junk shop – no arms and an inverted triangular seat;

when Deborah saw it (in those days she could still manage the stairs) she laughed and said, 'Oh darling, it's a birthing chair . . .' For a while I didn't feel quite the same about it, but in the end I decided that since no one would ever give birth in my bathroom it didn't matter too much. I spent a lot of care and more money than I could afford getting my bathroom just right, knocking down walls to make it bigger and so on; after all, it is where one tends the comfort and well-being of one's own body, so it needs to be an illuminated, spacious, calm place . . . This thought was suddenly not very cheering – for at that time there weren't very many well-lit, calm places in my life. And far too little of the lovely inner sense of space . . . Tasos: perceptive of him to see a contrast between what could pretentiously be described as my *postmodern* bathroom and me, rather than between it and this shabby old dowager of a building.

I said to myself that it was unlikely Tasos would get in touch with me again. And though he had scrupulously given me his phone number (a courtesy: 'Yes, you picked me up, our meeting was casual, one lonely evening – but I know your name and address so I shall give you mine'), I knew that any initiative would have to come from him. This didn't stop me thinking of him and wondering about him.

He did get in touch, though, a few weeks later. He telephoned me one afternoon and asked me rather formally if I was free to have dinner with him that night. I almost said that I was not free, oh what a pity, perhaps one day next week, Thursday maybe if you can manage it – that sort of thing. Playing hard to get. A rather austere and wise guardian angel put his hand on my shoulder: I said, yes, I am free, and yes, I should like to see you. Honesty. Generally speaking, all the little flirtations at the beginning of a love affair are really rather delicious, aren't they? Advance, retreat, my move, your move, will he, won't he: small rituals, part of a game whose rules you both know, a formalised pursuit (ah, but who is the quarry and who the hunter?), ending rapidly in blissful surrender. However, none of this seemed to apply to Tasos. My angel told me not to play around with him. In any case, it did not appear to be the start of a love affair so the question didn't arise (how lovely: *le mot juste*).

Once again Tasos slept on my sofa. He asked with a surprisingly tranquil directness, 'May I stay here tonight?' so that I answered equally simply 'Yes': no explanations, no questions. Had it been anyone else I would almost certainly have tried my luck, so to speak, but Tasos was different; this is why I did nothing when his bad dreams woke me that night – for I'm a light sleeper – but lay in bed listening to him muttering. I might have thought of going to wake him, making him a cup of tea or something, but the angel rapped me on the knuckles sharply and said, 'Don't pry, leave him alone.' In the morning he got up before me; I found him in the kitchen with the coffee ready, which made me inordinately happy although normally I'd be annoyed, outraged even, that anyone should mess around in my kitchen. 'I woke up early,' he said. 'I had claustrophobic nightmares.'

One sunlit Sunday morning later that spring he told me something about these dreams. 'There's a terrible sense of being hemmed in,' then, 'It's as if there wasn't any space to exist in any more. Sorry, that sounds rather silly.' It didn't seem particularly silly to me. To be more precise, it sounded horribly familiar: I know full well that awful mouth-drying, heart-lurching feeling of walls closing in. Generally though, as I see it, it's *people* who usurp your space, cabining and cribbing and confining you, edging you into a corner with their demands and expectations . . . Most of my life I've lived by myself, and this is perhaps why; right from the beginning Tasos's presence was comfortable because he seemed to make no assumptions about me. I doubt that he was particularly naive: merely he appeared to have his own version of the 'I am that I am' mantra.

What all this really amounted to was something like tentative, diffident friendship. The next time that Tasos woke me with his nightmares I did indeed feel diffident. I turned on the lamp and looked at the clock – it wasn't late, only two o'clock, for we had both been tired and had gone to bed early. I lay there and thought about things. Through the open window I could smell the orange blossom in the little park below, its sweet scent mingling with the quintessential urban aroma of petrol fumes and tired pavements. Tasos was tossing and turning restlessly, making little mewing sounds like a trapped animal. All my guardian angels appeared to be either off duty or unwilling to advise; the best thing seemed to be to do what came naturally. Thus I got up and went to Tasos, said, 'Move over,' and lay down beside him under the duvet. He woke, tensed slightly, said nothing. I put my arms around him and said, 'Hush, it's all right, it's all right, just go back to sleep again.'

If you are expecting me to say that violins played in the background, that we gazed into each other's eyes, that our lips met hungrily, that we slaked our passionate desire again and again, etc., etc., you'd be quite wrong. To begin with, it was too dark for us to see much of each other's faces. The only thing heard in the background was the distant rumble of traffic and the insistent, irritating drip of the kitchen tap whose washer needed replacing. And I did not kiss Tasos,

I simply held him close and stroked his hair gently until he relaxed. After a little while, in spite of the narrowness of the sofa, we both went to sleep. He slept first, his body warm and still against mine. I drifted between sleep and waking for a little longer, breathing in his scent, realising that what the orange trees outside really gave off was the sweet smell of hope.

VIII

'LE COEUR A SES RAISONS QUE LA RAISON NE CONNAIT POINT'

Your friends, my friends, perhaps one day our friends . . . Or is this unrealistic? Are 'our' friends in truth predominantly yours or mine, so that if we split up they will feel bound to take sides? First person pronouns matter here: if my friends do not care for *me*, then by definition they are not friends – merely the people among whom I live, my circle, acquaintances. 'A friend,' Fanny once said, 'is someone you can telephone in the middle of the night if the worst comes to the worst, knowing that their grumbling at being woken will be superficial, that they will respond freely to your need.' (It is annoying, of course, if one of your friends rings *you* in the middle of the night and wakes *me* up as well: the dynamics of friendship undergo some subtle shifts when couples begin to live together.) Joshua lived alone, however, and in the not so distant past Felix had more than once telephoned him at the miserable insomniac hour of three in the morning. But the other thing about friends is that they like to know the ins and outs of our lives . . . And Joshua, generous responder to late, late phone calls, was no exception.

'He's in love, Fan-Fan, that's the truth. Such a transparent little liar, says he isn't, can't imagine quite who he thinks is going to believe him. He *blushes*, Fanny.'

He shifted restlessly in his chair, cracked his finger joints (this was something that had always irritated Felix), lit a cigarette.

'It'll all end in tears before bedtime . . . Actually, tears after bedtime more likely, if you ask me.'

(In this Joshua was not far wrong: one night some time later tears were indeed shed, though as it happens they were not Felix's.)

'Oh darling, it can't be that bad.'

'Yes it is, it's worse. One more heartbreak just waiting to happen. People should stick to their own kind, it's a recipe for disaster.'

He got up and crossed to the window. Kind Fanny refrained from asking him not to twist the ends of the curtains where they were fraying.

'It's not that I particularly care who he gets involved with (though snapping and saying "Mind your own business" is *not* the way to talk to one's oldest friends), just that one does so hate to see him heading straight for trouble . . . And *someone*'s going to have to pick up the pieces and sweep up the mess and mop up the tears . . .'

'Just leave him be, darling. It really isn't your business, is it, nor mine either. And if it comes to sweeping and mopping I dare say we'll cope.'

You'd think, wouldn't you, that people might be glad when their friends fall in love (let's assume for the moment that Joshua's diagnosis was correct – after all, he knew Felix quite well). We often aren't glad though, there's frequently a slightly nose-out-of-joint undertone to our feelings and a little frisson of *schadenfreude* if things go wrong. A twinge of jealousy perhaps (although on second thoughts a milder word might really be better): at any rate, more than a twinge of discomfort as we recognise that we are suddenly excluded from the centre of our friend's life. Like most of us, Joshua preferred to deny such feelings: 'I can't help worrying that he's going to get hurt' is a rationalisation on a par with 'It's just that she's not at all the right kind of woman for him' (in either case, what presumption to imagine that we could even begin to judge). 'I can see the charms of the strong and silent type,' said Joshua, 'but the confused and silent type is quite another matter.' Of course, in the end we make the best of things; friendly affection finds its own level and if the new person becomes a permanent fixture in our friend's life we soon get used to the idea and may even grow fond of him or her.

However this may be, the fact remains that following the advent of Tasos into Felix's life Joshua was cross and Felix irritated with him. Both were in need of their steady confidante.

'The trouble is that they're not terribly fond of each other. I don't mean that they're not polite – a bit *too* polite actually, definitely frigid little smiles, awful conversations in the second person plural – but hackles rise, Deb, I can feel them both bristling, they sort of circle each other, one expects to see teeth bared any minute.'

'Never mind, lamb, they'll get used to one another. Here, thread this, will you, I always have difficulty with needles these days. Make the thread double so it's strong enough to take the weight.' They were sitting at her kitchen table making strings of vegetables – okra, aubergines, peppers – to dry in the sun.

'It's an act of faith, doing things for the future, isn't it,' she

said, 'even mundane everyday things like drying vegetables
for the winter. God willing, we shall all be alive and well
to enjoy them.'

'I don't have much faith, I'm scared of the future, Deb.
I don't know what will happen, I don't know anything'
(gloomily). 'I wish you had a crystal ball, Deborina mia, I
wish things were just a little bit less, um, *nebulous*.'

She said nothing for a few minutes, watched him as
he deftly threaded, his hands younger, less clumsy than
her own.

Then: 'Is it serious?'

'Perhaps. Probably. I don't know. Things aren't quite the
way everyone assumes.' (This conversation took place some
months before the winter night when tears were shed.)

Joshua had long since perfected what he called 'the Felix
tease'. Its latest refinement involved searching through the
religious calendars to find improbable saints, then suggesting
solicitously to Felix that in his current situation a candle
or two offered to them might not go amiss. The most
recent candidates were St Harmless, St Certain and St
Untrammelled: 'After all, darling, you may think he's
harmless but he *is* a teeny bit unsure, a little certainty
might not be unwelcome, don't you think? And I'm sure
you don't want any trammels or anything nasty like that
. . .' (St Harmless, St Certain and St Untrammelled, I might
add, were not Joshua's inventions; they really do exist, their
proper names being Akindynos, Vevaia and Anembodistos.)
Felix, who had never managed not to rise to the bait and
on occasion had actually been known to burst into tears
when teased too far, banged down his coffee cup and left,
slamming the door behind him.

'Josh is simply having a little sulk,' said Felix in answer to

her question, 'got his period, I suppose. I told him he bored
me, why not just go fuck himself, and he got all hurt. Well,
as far as I'm concerned he can simmer and sulk away for as
long as he likes. He's being insufferable, Deborah.'

'Fanny, he's so touchy, dry tinder is nothing in compari-
son, he flares up – and, I may say, gets very rude indeed –
at the slightest little tease. Not that he was ever famous for
his sense of humour, poor sweet, but recently he really is
taking his precious sensitivity a bit too far.'

Fanny (whom Felix always called Deborah: 'I *can't* call
you Fanny, darling') was a diplomatic peace-maker. Thus:
'Don't take him so seriously, my lamb, he can't help teasing,
if you don't pay too much attention he'll stop,' and, 'Darling,
come on, do be a bit kinder and leave him in peace, you
know he can't help being moody.' The dynamic shifts,
the rearrangement of the kaleidoscope patterns when a
new person is introduced into the picture are not always
easy at first.

Hurt feelings, thin skins, raised hackles, ruffled feathers:
how very much simpler life would be if everyone was equable
and not overly sensitive. But then again, whoever said that
life was meant to be simple . . . and a world full of stolid
souls would not be much fun. Hurt feelings do lead to a
certain edginess though, which has the annoying habit of
being catching, noxiously permeating other aspects of life,
beclouding relations other than those where the soreness
originally arose. Thus it happened that at dinner, a few
hours after one of Fanny's attempts to soothe Felix, Tasos
unwittingly touched a tender spot.

'I don't somehow think your friend Joshua likes me
very much.'

Felix shrugged. 'You don't like him much either.'

'When a person makes it quite clear from the beginning that he dislikes and distrusts you, it's not very conducive to liking.'

'Too bad.'

It takes time to know someone well enough to read the signals and understand when to let well alone; Tasos did not yet recognise the fractional tensing and tautening of Felix's body and thus continued.

'Is he your lover?'

Iciness. 'No. He is not my lover. I haven't got a lover. That's the truth. But perhaps that isn't what interests you, you're wanting to know do I go to bed with him, well, in that case the answer is yes, on and off, from time to time I do. Of course I do. I like him. I've known him for aeons. He's a friend. We have a little fuck when we feel like it. He's not my lover. OK, have we got that straight now?'

'Yes.'

'Do you have any objections, maybe?' (extremely icy).

A pause while he considered. Then, mildly, 'No, I don't think so.'

Anyone else might have jumped in without a moment's hesitation and protested in tones of unconvincing amazement, 'Who, me? No, what an idea, of course not.' Tasos's judiciousness was to some extent reassuring, even if not quite enough to prevent Felix from feeling miserably at odds with everything. Their meal proceeded in a rather subdued manner. Felix crumbled his bread in irritated distraction. Luckily on this occasion Tasos's feelings were not liable to hurt and he was not infected by Felix's touchiness; he thus watched him, waited a bit, then said:

'Why are you so angry? I asked because I wanted to know, and you answered. What's wrong with that? You yourself told me, Felix, that words are for making sense of things with . . .'

'So you think I made sense?'

'Yes, I think you made perfect sense, it was a remarkably clear and precise exposition actually.'

The following day was a working day for both of them; they thus said goodnight fairly soon after this and made their separate ways home. 'Oh God, another sleepless night,' thought Felix, who'd been having some bad ones. He debated whether to read a bit, then turned off the lamp and lay on his back thinking. Long before, in a non-teasing spirit, Joshua had given him a small Coptic icon, a winged, spear-bearing angel with bright, primitive, determined black eyes; Felix hung it in his bedroom and generally kept a nightlight burning beneath it in a saucer of water. The faint flicker of candlelight reflected in all his mirrors was a soothing accompaniment to sleep and a comfort in wakefulness. ('When I lay me down to sleep, fourteen angels watch do keep' – the child's version, thought Felix.)

The phone rang.

'Felix. Did I wake you, were you asleep? . . . Good.' A long pause. 'Listen, I didn't mean to make you feel you had to explain anything . . . You didn't want to talk about it, did you, well, I just wanted to say sorry if you felt I was too curious.'

Felix's turn to pause. Then: 'Ah, Tasos, Tasos, not being a cat you're allowed to be curious – oh dear, that's something very English, I'll explain another time – but anyway I'm sorry too, I was in a prickly mood all day, just don't pay too much attention.'

'I won't, all right, goodnight, sleep well, sweet dreams.'

All sorts of things find their own level in life if we can

only refrain from interfering and allow them to do so. If we are able to still all the clamorous, petty expectations, to cease fretting and to wait receptively, then – for good or for bad – things will flow along whatever channel fate or fortune or chance has ordained. And, in more mundane terms, ruffled feathers will be smoothed, old friends and new friends (lovers maybe) will come to accept each other more or less gracefully. And of course, when we are calm we find rest. For one reason or another Tasos's phone call salved Felix's soreness. 'Goodnight, sleep well, sweet dreams': a little everyday ritual phrase of the kind that is offered and received without much conscious thought, yet also of the kind that is offered in warmth – to a lover, to a young child. Felix was tired and was thinking more of the first part of this conversation as he turned off the lamp once more. Nevertheless, the warm words took effect and there is no doubt at all that for once Felix slept well.

IX

ΜΙΑ ΖΩΗ ΠΡΟΣΠΑΘΩ ΝΑ ΠΕΘΑΝΩ
ΚΑΙ ΚΑΘΕ ΜΕΡΑ ΞΑΝΑΓΕΝΝΙΕΜΑΙ

ALL MY LIFE I'VE BEEN TRYING TO DIE
AND EVERY DAY I'M BORN AGAIN

Graffiti, Maroussi, Athens

Most of your friends do not really approve when you get involved with a married man. It may well be that you don't quite approve yourself either, but it happens . . . Of course, if you have any sense at all you just get on with it without telling your friends. And from this point of view a married man has certain advantages: apart from the late afternoon hours that are so sacred – that all too brief little magic time between the end of the working day and the beginning of the evening proper (for the Greek evening does not begin much before nine o'clock) – the rest of your social life continues as usual. You frequent your regular haunts, meet your friends, go to the theatre with them perhaps (though sometimes cutting it rather fine and arriving late, so that they are standing on the pavement glancing at their watches impatiently, debating whether to leave your ticket at the box office for you). Your more perceptive friends may notice how well you are looking, even if they are too tactful to comment. But, but, but . . . Those magic hours are indeed much too brief . . . A married man has many disadvantages.

'So why did I not keep away?' thought Leonora a couple

of weeks after meeting Tasos. And the answer of course is that age-old human *cri de coeur*, that justification for everything, that plea for forgiveness: 'I couldn't help it . . . ' It was not that she didn't know he was married. To begin with he wore a wedding ring – a broad band of gold, the old-fashioned kind that proclaims commitment. Then, too, he had made it clear during one of their early conversations, one of those tentative little exchanges where what is really being said is quite other than the apparent subject; on this occasion the apparent subject was for some reason cats. 'I prefer dogs actually,' he said, then, in answer to her question, 'No, I haven't had a dog since I was a child, I live in a flat, you see . . . And anyway, my wife doesn't like the idea of pet animals in the house, she feels they're rather dirty . . .' And so the words were said and Leonora noted them: 'my wife'. I imagine that she also unconsciously noted some of the other things that were being said (for there is no doubt that when people are attracted to one another their antennae become extraordinarily sensitive): 'I do not have what I want,' and 'I live confined in a space which is not comfortable,' and 'My wife does not much like the fact that I am a living male animal.' Needless to say, Tasos was quite unaware of what he was saying, and equally needless to say it was a foregone conclusion that they would very rapidly end up in bed. If we are charitable we could say that neither of them could help it.

Appropriating another woman's husband contravenes all the canons of the sisterhood, as one of Leonora's friends pointed out firmly. For in the end the temptation to tell someone about Tasos and say his name aloud was too strong for Leonora to resist and thus she confided in first one and then another friend (it does indeed require a fair degree of self-possession to remain absolutely silent when you are in love). 'If she wants him, then she ought to value him more,' snapped Leonora, knowing as she said it that this particular bit of childishness was unworthy of her. 'She doesn't own him.' (We'll come back to this idea later.) Anyway, there is of course a difference between the general and the specific: 'another woman's husband' is one thing, gentle, ardent, hesitant, smiling Tasos quite another.

Ardent and smiling – understandably. Hesitant? Well, why not? I cannot see that there is any rule that prevents middle-aged men from being just as unsure and confused as anyone else, though there are certainly cultural conventions that on the whole require them to conceal such feelings. There are other conventions too which weigh more heavily on the married lover than on the single one . . . Foremost among these is the necessity of switching rapidly between modes: you get up from your girlfriend's bed, wash carefully and dress, you kiss her goodbye, check scrupulously that there are no tell-tale long blonde hairs (long red hairs in Tasos's case) on your clothes, you go home . . . And then you must enter into the 'How was your day?' or 'What's for dinner?' type of conversation. Moreover, bed as well as board is shared by your lawful wife (Tasos was perhaps not flexible enough to perceive that the illicit might add a little extra piquancy to the licit; if you don't feel this way, then there's not much to be done except perhaps sometimes to watch a late, late film on television until she's safely asleep). I dare say Tasos would have got better at all this with practice, yet the fact remains that it is not really natural for happy lovemaking to be followed by so sudden a wrench; if for whatever reason you must part from your lover, then it would be a lot more comfortable to remain quietly by yourself, savouring the peace within you. The stress of such forced reorientation – by the end it was almost daily – was a source of great anguish for Tasos. Perhaps it might have helped had he been able to speak of it. (Perhaps, on second thoughts, Leonora was indeed quite sensible to confide in her friends.) Much later, as it happens, Tasos did speak of some of these things when he was lucky enough to find a sympathetic, intelligent listener. By then, however, he was divorced and living alone. And even then he spoke stumblingly, so that in fact more of his anguish and uncertainty and failure and despair was communicated by what was left unsaid than by what was said.

But to go back. If you are not in the habit of articulating your feelings – even to yourself – your vocabulary tends to be rather limited, so that when from the fullness of your heart you attempt to tell the other person what you feel it comes out sounding like a cliché. What Tasos said to Leonora one day when they had more time together than usual and had gone to walk on a winter beach, in search of space and exhilarated by the icy blustering wind, was, 'All my life I think I've been half dead and with you I am alive.' Poor man – we should not doubt that the feeling was genuine even if the words were threadbare. Nor should we jump to facile conclusions and assume patronisingly from our superior position that all he was trying to express was merely the sense of great sexual happiness after some rather lean years (though clearly this too was involved). In any case, Leonora did not analyse his words but simply turned to him and put her arms around him. And they stood thus for some time, warm and still in a close embrace, oblivious of the cold and the wind and the stinging spray from the sea. But even such private and intense moments are grounded in reality.

59

Leonora had left her gloves in the car and a little while later said, 'My hands are cold.' 'Put them in my pockets,' he suggested after kissing them tenderly, and she did so, only to feel his keys, to become aware once more, with a jolt, of another life, another front door to be opened, another person awaiting him. (And he, as he opened that other door a couple of hours later, suddenly realised that in his pockets were still some of the shells that she had collected.) The little jarring awkwardnesses of adultery intrude when we least expect them.

Married men do indeed have many disadvantages: they belong with someone else (this is the correct preposition). Unless or until one or other of the partners is prepared to get out the sharpest knife and sever in one fell swoop all the subtle bonds of belonging that have become so densely interwoven over the years, these ties remain – sometimes with a degree of elasticity that makes the discomfort not too chafing, sometimes so sticky and constricting that they hurt (and the more you struggle, the more you become enmeshed). Tasos, struggling, found himself unable to disentangle his own wishes, far less all the strands of familiarity, hostility, pity that constituted his marriage. 'She doesn't own me,' he said to himself in a moment of guilt, yet this incontrovertible fact – as anyone a little wiser could have told him – changed nothing. For what she does own, always, is the inalienable right to make certain claims on you: care, consideration, courtesy.

Was it then only his marriage that was the great stumbling block? This is what Leonora's friends assumed, telling her with varying degrees of crudity that Tasos, like so many others, was simply having his cake and eating it; Leonora, knowing this wasn't true, preferred for a long time to imagine that everything was his wife's fault. Tasos, too, increasingly uncertain of himself and less and less able to find any kind of solution, tended to feel that it was marriage that was the living death. Neither of them possessed enough clarity to illuminate the misunderstandings that began to arise; both were unconsciously led astray by that most pernicious of popular beliefs, *love by itself is enough*, without pausing to define what love might be, without considering that *amor vincit omnia* can only be true if love is based on knowledge, that knowledge, understanding, tolerance take time. The results were inevitable: an impartial observer could have predicted the failures and pain and misery which began to cast a strain on a web not yet strong enough to bear them.

So the answer is no, of course not, it was something much more complicated than the simple fact of his marriage that led Tasos and Leonora to part. Long afterwards, when it had all ended, both gradually came to realise a little of what had gone wrong. Into Leonora's mind came the word 'cowardice' – applied to both of them – and she understood that, insuperable obstacle though a wife may be, she cannot in all honesty be blamed for everything; to the perennial angry thought, 'She stabbed him in the balls,' was added the miserable recognition, 'I stabbed him in the back.' And Tasos's sympathetic listener – never a very great partisan of wives in general or of Tasos's wife in particular – held him close one night and said with gentleness, 'It was not she who did it to you, you did it to yourself.'

There are no doubt problems when one lover is married to someone else. It is conceivable that if Tasos had been single everything might have worked out very differently. 'If' and 'if only' are not words that lead along the firmest paths of life though, not words that can bear the weight of much solid, fertile reality. If everything had been different? If the Archduke had not been assassinated that summer day? If . . . ? No, useless, things happen the way they do. And who can say what is best? Tasos and Leonora separately passed through near deathly despair, and separately – such is the insistence of the forces of life – each in the end found a small, undramatic opportunity for rebirth.

X

PAIN IS EVERYTHING
AND EVERYTHING IS PAIN

Graffiti (in English), Exarcheia, Athens

The trouble with pain is that it does tend to overflow from one bit of the body to another, from one part of life to another. It requires a kind of discipline to control it, to limit the pain to one area. And of course before you can exercise any kind of control you have to recognise where the pain is coming from: this is more easily done with toothache than with soul-ache. Discipline, in any case, isn't a very well-liked word these days; it has some rather unpleasantly authoritarian overtones, quite apart from the fact that several decades of half-baked psychology in the popular press have led to a curious confusion between self-discipline and the kind of over-control that is tantamount to being uptight (dreadful fate). Nevertheless, without a reasonably strong dose of discipline neither the craftsman nor the athlete would be able to achieve very much. Nor indeed would perfectly ordinary men and women be so successful at taking a deep breath and coping with the perfectly ordinary upheavals of life. The cost of such coping – the amount of pain involved – depends in part on whether the discipline being applied has a small 'd', is supple, flexible, graceful, or whether it has an extremely large capital 'D' and is rigidly strait-laced.

Thinking of corsets, we might note that Marianna had the kind of *belle époque* figure that would have suited tight lacing: a full bosom, a small waist, well-rounded haunches and slim legs. It's not the sort of figure that is much seen in fashion photographs, yet to most people – consciously or unconsciously – it instantly proclaims 'feminine' (followed perhaps by 'female', 'sexy'; for it's the sort of figure that evokes wolf-whistles from building sites and pinches or worse in crowded Athens buses). It is never easy to disentangle quite why people are the way they are and I certainly do not want to labour any point about women as mere sex objects or anything like that; yet I think we can assume that somewhere, somehow, for many people there is a tenuous connection between the way others view them and their self-image. And it would probably be fair to say that some part of Marianna's sense of herself as 'feminine', interpreted culturally as 'passive', 'dependent', stemmed from the simple fact that in her body subcutaneous fat was distributed in shapely curves of apparently extreme voluptuousness.

Actually, by temperament Marianna was not really passive at all. Her husband, in the early days of their marriage, used to maintain (only half joking) that in her was to be seen one of the greatest Prime Ministers that the country had never had. And it is true that her organisational talents were rather wasted running a household consisting of just the two of them. Her misfortune, perhaps, was that she had not been born ten years later, or to parents ten years younger, or even in a city ten times larger than the small and conservative provincial town where she grew up. For had all these things been different it is possible that someone might have considered her worth educating properly, worth steering towards a career, so that even if she had not ended up as Prime Minister she would at least have had wider horizons within which to make her life, more confidence in her own abilities. I might go as far as to say what a pity she did not have ten siblings, since it is probable that she would then have received a more liberal upbringing. As it was, she was the much-loved, over-protected only child of elderly parents; they raised her in a way that was already somewhat old-fashioned – she was that rarity, a virgin when she married – and instilled into her some deeply pernicious views of what constitutes decent womanly behaviour. This too may have had something to do with the appearance of passivity and dependence.

A lot of long-accepted truths tend to be cynically questioned these days rather than taken as self-evident, yet in Marianna's world it was still more or less universally acknowledged that a woman is in want of a husband. What was never acknowledged was that, once achieved, the marriage might not last for ever . . . I've often wondered, incidentally, why people set such store by photographs of their own weddings – after all, if you are present in the flesh yourself and your spouse is also very much present in the flesh beside you, then why on earth should you need a framed portrait of yourselves walking down the aisle together? However, weddings are weddings, conventions are comforting, and on her bedside table Marianna duly kept a large picture of herself, shy and white-gowned, holding the arm of Tasos, serious and dark-suited. This photograph was for years never really *looked at* by either of them, but it remained in place between the lamp and the alarm clock and the box of paper handkerchiefs, a solid reassuring confirmation of the apparently safe, solid bonds of marriage.

We seem to have amassed quite a few appearances already: apart from apparent passivity, we have apparent security, apparent voluptuousness. I know and you know and Marianna came to know the hard way that even the most seemingly secure bonds can fray alarmingly, that marriage is not automatically for ever. (Appearances may be 'kept up' – but that's another matter.) After many years of apparent (yes: once again) tranquillity, her marriage disintegrated; the familiar unquestioned routine of co-existence wavered for a while, then petered out, leaving in its place an ugly void. A painful night thus arrived when suddenly Marianna had the bed to herself; before turning off the lamp she looked at the photograph as if seeing it for the first time, then turned and lay face down across the whole width of the bed and wept in comfortless misery, again for the first time in years (Marianna had taught herself as a child never to cry and had shed no tears since, not even at her parents' funerals). The following morning she removed the photograph from its frame and slowly and methodically tore it into the tiniest of fragments. This was the extent of what she called 'loss of control'.

Now, I have no particular wish to pry into Marianna's private life, yet I have to say that the third appearance – the sensual promise of her curvaceous body – was also deceptive. The box of paper tissues by the bed is indicative. For whereas the average sensualist glories in the intrinsic blissful messiness of human coupling, Marianna found it distasteful. It did not occur to her that it was anything other than appropriate to lay a towel on the bed before any marital embrace – 'to keep the sheets clean'; for some reason Tasos accepted this without remark and, although with time he managed to persuade her not to leap up and hurry to the bathroom immediately afterwards, he never succeeded in making her relax before she had washed. Early on in their marriage he had indeed suggested that washing might very well wait until morning (getting up more than once a night for this purpose *is* a trifle restless and fidgety); in those days her blank incomprehension had amused him and made him feel expansively tender towards her. However, such tenderness inevitably waned, their lovemaking throughout the years being invariably followed by a certain tension as Marianna silently counted the minutes that must elapse before she was allowed to get up. Clearly this was not a very happy state of affairs. Perhaps Tasos might have overcome Marianna's reserve if he had understood that feeling clean means feeling in control and had been able to give her more confidence. This, though, he was unable to do. And in the end I don't think either of them can be blamed for this failure.

Might things have been easier if they had had children? Hard to tell: I doubt that it would have made much difference to their essential lack of harmony, yet Marianna might have been happier. Each suspected – wrongly as it happens – that the other blamed him or her for their lack of children. Neither knew which of them was infertile. Tasos, reasonably enough, had at the beginning suggested consulting a doctor; Marianna had not said no outright but had not agreed either, and somehow, tacitly, the question was postponed. And the years passed. The fact is that Marianna felt that it must be her fault, was deeply reluctant to have this confirmed officially, and then felt twice as much to blame.

In any case Marianna found gynaecological examinations unpleasant, uncomfortable and somehow humiliating. I have to say I sympathise a bit with this, specially in view of the particular gynaecologist that she visited for her regular check-ups . . . ('We never wanted children,' she told him sharply, 'I leave all that to my husband,' and he asked no further questions. Marianna considered herself truthful, yet – like most of us – was well able to lie fluently in what she obscurely thought of as self-defence.) And although a highly competent and fairly sensitive woman gynaecologist practised within walking distance of her home, who might perhaps have been able to elicit the truth, Marianna chose to go across town to a distinguished male consultant whose patients had never seemed much more to him than anonymous reproductive tracts, functioning or not functioning, and who thus had never paused to consider that the parts which he poked and prodded might actually be attached to women with feelings. It had never occurred to him, for example, that when an ice-cold metal speculum is plunged into your vagina you cannot help flinching and tensing – if the instrument is at least room-temperature or slightly warm from the steriliser, then the patient is more likely to relax. He had also never questioned the received dogma that the only way to examine a woman is on a gynaecological chair with stirrups; Marianna's neighbour – whom I knew and respected – never used stirrups and always said that they make women feel powerless and exposed: 'You can examine them perfectly well if they lie on their sides with their knees drawn up,' she maintained, 'and they're much more relaxed this way.' So why did Marianna persist in consulting someone who made her feel so uncomfortable? Well, I'm afraid we are back with appearances being deceptive: the man *looked* avuncular and kindly, rosy-complexioned and silver-haired, softly spoken, with plump, well-kept, manicured hands, and Marianna – along with a host of other women – was taken in.

But in any case the pain which invaded Marianna after

her marriage started falling to pieces was an ache of the mind rather than of the fallopian tubes. So unaccustomed was this ache, though, that it took her some time to recognise it for what it was. At first she ignored Tasos's air of sleek well-being; then she thought to herself how incomprehensible males really are ('Oh well, if that's what he wants, let him have it'); then – too late – alarm bells started sounding. Now that Tasos showed no signs whatsoever of requiring it, Marianna began to wonder if she had been wise to keep her well-laundered towel folded up in the linen cupboard for so much of the time recently. She watched her sleeping husband and saw a secretive, unfamiliar stranger whose life had moved out of her reach.

Marianna had a surprisingly sharp tongue. And, as she fought to regain control, she used it, withering, belittling, blindly seeking to render him powerless and thus neutralise the threat. There's not really much necessity to describe in any detail the terrible clashes that ensued; all that need be said is that they led to the kind of hostility which made Marianna increasingly acid and Tasos increasingly unresponsive. She felt helpless in the face of his morose silence, hated this sense of helplessness, found herself goading him just to provoke some reaction, any reaction. And when he then got up, said curtly, 'There's no point in all this,' and left the room, closing the door aggressively quietly behind him, frightening pain began to take over. She tried to say to herself, 'This is just a phase, he'll get over it' (note the pronoun), and several times took refuge in the most extraordinarily unnecessary domestic tasks (cleaning out the kitchen cupboards at 11 o'clock one Sunday evening, for example, as if this calming ritual would somehow restore normality). I rather tend to think it is happy families that are, each one, unique while unhappy families drearily resemble each other: a long recitation of Marianna's and Tasos's hurt and fear and anger and loneliness would probably be sadly familiar to far too many of us.

Another sad and familiar truth: no amount of discipline ultimately allows us control over another person – the more we try, the worse things become. This is sometimes hard to recognise at first. In the end, of course, when he has actually removed his books from the shelves and his clothes from the cupboards, you have no choice but to accept that he has made a decision by himself, for himself, and is leaving you. And it is at this point that the pain spills over, swamping every part of your being, making you no longer able to distinguish which bit hurts. You may begin to wonder if you are actually physically ill; like Marianna, you may find that suddenly being alone at night makes you panic in case you have a heart attack *with no one there to help you* – whereupon of course your heart instantly starts palpitating wildly. It is now that you need every ounce of discipline that you possess in order to salvage your pride, to keep a semblance of control. And if, like poor Marianna, your pride, your discipline and your self-control are of the uptight variety, who in your distress could be cruel enough to blame you?

XI

I MISS THE COMFORT IN BEING SAD

Graffiti (in English), Piazza Navone, Rome

I don't know whether it serves some obscure evolutionary purpose or whether it merely indicates an innate masochistic streak, but it is noticeable that human beings have a great capacity for putting up with the most uncomfortable circumstances. Alternatively of course it might be the expression of a very laudable pious resignation. Or maybe, less optimistically, it is merely a matter of sloth or cowardice: too much trouble perhaps to try to change one's circumstances, rather frightening to embark on a voyage away from the familiar discomfort and into the unknown. Suppose, after all, that the unknown turns out to be even worse than the known . . .

What I am really saying is that although Tasos's marriage was never particularly happy it was for many years unthinkable for him to consider alternatives. Surprising perhaps that he had remained a faithful husband for so long (sloth, cowardice, some essential timidity?), since quite clearly among the obvious sources of unhappiness was an almost total lack of sexual harmony between him and his wife. Yet beneath this, I rather think, lay an even deeper level of discomfort. These things are invariably somewhat tenuous and hard to express, but crudely speaking what was perhaps lacking in both Tasos and Marianna was any of the sort of knowledge of self or other which allows people to develop a flow of communication. (Tasos much later once mentioned to Felix that over the portals of the school which as a child he had entered day after day was inscribed the Delphic prescription 'Know Thyself'; Felix made no comment, though at that point in their acquaintance he was wondering rather a lot to what extent people know their true inclinations, but it did occur to him that Tasos had not taken this instruction to heart. "Lord, we know what we are, but know not what we may be" he quoted to himself and went on wondering – about the first half of this statement in particular.) I was about to say that the inability to apprehend and communicate with another person beyond the everyday level is rather like being tone-deaf or colour-blind – but on second thoughts I think I'm wrong, for it is not in fact completely incurable. When Tasos finally met Felix and was encouraged step by step as it were, he began to manage a little better. It is a handicap which is exacerbated, though, if both partners in a marriage suffer from it. But even such intrinsic silence can come to seem familiar.

And the sense of familiarity is of extreme importance to the human animal, no doubt about it. Have you noticed, for example, that when people eat regularly in the same restaurant they tend to head for the same table each time (and to feel a half-conscious sense of outrage if this table is already taken when they arrive)? Or have you ever wondered why when two people regularly share a bed they tend to take it for granted that each has his or her own side? Patterns and routines and well-trodden paths are what most people's lives consist of. So I suppose that we shouldn't really be surprised that all the familiar patterns of discomfort and unhappiness became woven into the known fabric of Tasos's life and tolerated for years on end. Sadness can perhaps begin to resemble an embracing old armchair into which to sink – or better still, an easy, well-worn (even if a trifle frowsty) garment to don each day instead of stripping naked and facing the elements.

Now I don't particularly want to take a superior moral stance and say in scornful tones, 'How pathetically timid,' yet the truth is that Tasos was not much given to facing the elements, was more the sort of person whose life tends to be characterised by a very great disinclination to take risks. It is safer to wear a seat belt, to hold the handrail and keep to the path (strait and narrow maybe, though called in the Greek New Testament strait and sad); it is wiser to find steady employment – to work your way up, for example, through the grades of a stable civil service career; it is more prudent to get married and settle down, to sleep each night on your own fixed side of the bed. If sadness is involved, well, you get accustomed to it.

If you had come across Tasos during these years of his life I doubt whether you would have given him a second thought. You might have sat opposite him on the train, of course – one of those moments when you've forgotten your book and there's nothing better to do – and idly observed him as he read his newspaper. 'Good hands,' you might have thought (this was one of the first things that Leonora noticed about him), or 'rather nice hair' (Felix spotted this at once), and your gaze would have wandered elsewhere. If you were a tiny bit fey you might have felt that from him emanated very faintly the smell of quiet despair (though Felix detected something quite different). The chances are, though, that if you had registered Tasos's presence at all you would have dismissed him as one of the ordinary, decent, respectable, predictable citizens.

Ordinary people have feelings, don't forget . . . And, albeit rather blindly, Tasos did start straying. 'A mid-life crisis,' various well-meaning friends told Marianna when he fell quite helplessly in love with Leonora, 'the male menopause,' and other such idiocies. 'It's his age, that's all, he's just having a final fling': a predictable, even conventional, sort of outbreak. (The apparent pessimism of this word 'final' may at first seem puzzling: after all, Tasos was not so very much over fifty at the time and one might have expected his friends to assume that he had a couple of decades at least of potential flings in front of him. These were family friends, however, rather than people who felt special warmth for Tasos as an individual, and what was implied was that Marianna would be wise to permit him this one adventure and then call him firmly to heel and secure the leash.) Tasos indeed felt rejuvenated (once again, predictably enough); nevertheless some of Marianna's cutting words presumably scored a hit, for when things started going badly with Leonora he found himself thinking with sadness, 'I am too old for her . . .' 'So how old was she?' asked Felix when Tasos began to tell him about it, then, smiling faintly, changed the subject on discovering that Leonora was little more than a year younger than himself. But Felix at least had long known that age does not bear much relation to anything. Thus, 'Tasos, Tasos, crying has to do with feelings, it's got nothing to do with how old you are,' he said one emotional night some time later as he cradled a weeping and apologetic Tasos in his arms ('Oh God, I'm sorry, I shouldn't be crying like a baby, I'm sorry . . .'). In fact the cradling and the gentle comforting rocking rather belied his words – being the age-old movements used to soothe an infant – but since neither of them noticed this it didn't matter: in any case, the painful sobs were quieted.

Among the many other patterns of life are those created by definitions, and among the most deeply rooted of all definitions are those concerning gender. We all know that they vary according to culture and in some societies are quite wonderfully fluid, while in others – such as the milieu inhabited for so long by Tasos – there is not much elasticity: it is taken for granted that women are 'feminine' and men 'masculine' and that there are sets of behaviour appropriate to each category. Crying, for example, is largely seen as the prerogative of women and children; a man may perhaps shed a few brief manly tears under the pressure of a great and publicly recognised grief, but crying in bed with Felix does *not* come under such a heading: indeed, a great many people would consider being in bed with Felix not very manly in the first place. (Some of these facile assumptions are indeed deeply rooted: Tasos, in spite of finding Felix's bed a comfortable place to be, nevertheless later chided him for crying too easily, and Felix, still nervous of displeasing, generously forbore to remind Tasos of his own tears.) However, it is not merely that the conventions require adult men not to cry: the fact is that, unless you are lucky enough to have close, warm friends whom you trust, it is generally speaking socially easier to admit to feeling utterly miserable if you are a woman than if you are a man. And the kind of misery that you cannot admit to does turn rather easily into an awful vicious circle of inadequacies and uncertainties . . . It would probably be fair to say that the faint but persistent whiff of despair emanating from Tasos in his pre-Felix days had something to do with the disparity between such feelings and the prescribed masculine role he felt obliged to play.

75

Unhappiness of this sort compounded by silence leads to an ever-increasing desperate sense of being trapped.

This in turn may have something to do with whatever it was that attracted Tasos to Felix in the first place. I imagine that what he was originally seeking was probably ease of a spiritual rather than a genital variety. Felix, you see, felt able to say quite matter-of-factly things like, 'I was feeling very lonely tonight,' or, 'My lover left me six months ago and it still hurts,' or, 'Well, if you really want to know, I drink myself to sleep sometimes so that I won't cry myself to sleep – I know drink is not so good for the complexion in the long term, but in the short term nights of crying are quite *catastrophic* for my looks.' To Tasos the open simplicity of such statements was at first astounding and then somehow remarkably comforting. With Felix none of the usual pretences appeared to be required. Felix and his strange apartment in any case seemed so far removed from the everyday life of Tasos's experience that words could be said which never could have been uttered elsewhere. And words as we know have great liberating power . . .

Thus it was that Tasos managed at long last to depart from the sad, strait, narrow (straight and narrow?) path. To anyone casually seeing the two of them together it might have appeared that Felix – so much younger, so much lighter in manner, so much slighter in figure – was the dependent; things are rarely as clear-cut as this, but all the same I suspect that if the relationship was one of dependence then it may very well have been the other way round. However this may be, in the relaxed atmosphere that Felix seemed able to provide Tasos gradually shrugged off his old, familiar, shabby robe of sadness and found himself much more comfortable without it.

XII

ΑΝΤΙ ΤΗΣ ΣΙΩΠΗΣ

INSTEAD OF SILENCE

Graffiti, KAT, Athens

This in the end is perhaps the most interesting piece of graffiti of all. For it does nothing less than explain in three succinct words the great impulse that leads to the writing of words on walls: *Kev loves Abigail*, for example, or *Death to all capitalists*, or whatever probable or improbable thought the writer can no longer bear to hold in silence in his heart. You could say graffiti are one of the humblest expressions of the perennial human need to reach across the boundaries between self and other. We touch and we speak: a confirmation that we are not alone in the speechless, chilly, silent dark but form part of the great warm sprawling communion of saints and sinners. In a word, communication. If all else fails, write it on a wall . . .

On their way out to eat in their local taverna Tasos and Felix came across a new piece of graffiti – *Set fire to the parrot* – and debated its meaning.

'Anyway, what makes people write such strange things on walls?' asked Tasos.

'Haven't you ever written anything on a wall?'

'No, of course not.'

'Not even anything political? Not "Britain out of Cyprus" in the days of your youth or whatever the current slogan was?'

'No. Why, have you?'

'Yes. Not anything political. What I wrote was, well, anyway it was something my father called "unspeakably vulgar". Actually it wasn't vulgar at all – people like him can never call things by their proper names. It was just very obscene and perfectly speakable, though I don't think this is the right place to tell you in case a sudden silence falls and someone understands English. Wait, I'll whisper it in your ear . . .' (Slight involuntary change of expression on Tasos's face, slight blush on Felix's.) 'My career as a graffitist was singularly undistinguished though, began and ended there as a matter of fact, I got caught in the act just as I was standing back to admire my work and was fined for defacing public property . . . A bit embarrassing, except that my parents were so cringingly embarrassed and ashamed that I ended up feeling defiant more than anything else. The fine was supposed to pay for washing it off, but whatever they spent the money on it wasn't that, I'd used a particularly indelible yellow paint and it took ages for the rain to make it fade, my father had to drive home from work a different way to avoid seeing it. Actually in a way it was rather shame-making, Tasos, for you see the awful thing is I was so drunk that I spelt the most important bit of it wrong.'

'What on earth made you want to write it in the first place?'

'I don't know. Not ever being able to say the things I was thinking. Unhappiness. Loneliness. Something of that sort I suppose. Maybe also a little bit of the childish desire to shock. You don't approve, do you.'

A slight smile. 'Well . . . I dare say you can be forgiven for your youthful misdemeanours, Felix. But no, I don't really think it's a terribly good idea to write things like that on walls – you make people read them who maybe ought not to read them, I don't know, schoolchildren or something.'

'Oh, for God's sake, Tasos, they're only *words*. Either you know what they mean – in which case you've already imagined such things even if you haven't done them, or you don't understand at all, have no idea what they mean – in which case they can't possibly do you any harm. Anyway, in the first place I don't make a habit of writing obscenities on walls, and in the second place I was seventeen and they were liberating words, I *needed* to write them and I'm glad I got drunk enough to do it, and in the third place don't be so ridiculously bourgeois and parrot such inane received opinions.'

'I *am* bourgeois, Felix' (gently).

'And in the fourth place I'm over-reacting and that was very rude of me. Sorry. If you like I'll go and write "*mea culpa*" on the wall outside.'

'It's all right, there's no need.'

Felix took even longer than usual in the bathroom that night, having waited till Tasos had finished with it. The following morning Tasos found the mirror over the basin adorned with a large parrot drawn with the red felt-tipped pen that Felix used for marking his pupils' exercise books: the parrot sat on a sort of bonfire of flames, from its beak issued the words '*Mea maxima culpa*' and beneath it was written The Felix Bird. Tasos found the red pen, erased the 'l' in Felix and substituted an 'n'. 'English spelling never was my strong point, even when sober,' he explained as he became aware of Felix looking over his shoulder. Then, with great deliberation, he erased the words coming from the parrot's beak and in their place carefully wrote, 'One thing I know, that I know nothing.' 'There,' he said, 'that's better.' Felix put his arms round Tasos's waist, buried his face in the back of Tasos's neck. For a minute or so they remained thus without speaking, then proceeded to finish getting up, to have breakfast, to set off to work. When Felix got home that afternoon, slightly late, Tasos was already there watching the news; in the bathroom the mirror was wiped clean. Comment seemed unnecessary, though the silence was not uncomfortable. Both knew that the mirror graffiti had been an odd act of communication. An apology on one side, an apologia on the other perhaps.

A week or so later the conversation turned to the teaching of languages. Tasos reminisced about his first English teacher, a grotesquely ugly, lame maiden lady of uncertain age and sweet temper.

'She seems to have been a good teacher at any rate,' said Felix.

'She was, she had a sort of boundless childlike enthusiasm which was catching, for some reason she made you want to please her.'

'I'm sure you were a model pupil, eager to learn, not like my current lot' (smiling).

'Oh well, I was young and innocent . . .' (also smiling).

'The kids I teach may be young but one could hardly call them innocent. Tasos, listen,' serious once more, 'were you really so innocent? I mean, if you had seen my bit of drunken graffiti would you really and truly not have had the slightest little *inkling* of what it meant?'

'I don't quite think my English would have been up to it in those days, Felix.'

'Come on, you know that's not what I'm talking about.'

A slow smile. 'All right. I probably would have been terribly shocked to see it in writing but yes, I would have understood what it meant.'

'Ah.' Felix considered the implications of this. Then, in more flippant mode, 'Oh dear, now that we seem to be getting rather *truthful* all of a sudden I'd better confess something. It was terribly unfair of me to accuse you of being middle class, Tasos, because actually although I may not look it right now this minute that's exactly what I am myself.' (Since it was a public holiday Felix was what he called *en déshabillé*, in other words wearing a flowing indigo-coloured West African robe.)

'I know,' cheerfully enough. 'But why does it have to be a confession or an accusation? Does it matter? Can't it just be a simple fact?'

'It is, of course it is . . . only there are some *aspects* of facts that you run away from – or you do if you're me – and that's why I ended up living here.' An uncharacteristically long pause.

'What are you thinking?'

'Whether to give you a lovely romantic version of why I came to live in Greece or whether, since we're being truthful, to tell you the real reason.'

Tasos waited, said nothing.

'It was because of a person.'

'I wondered.'

'No, not at all what you're thinking, a very unromantic person, a dignitary of the church actually . . . and don't go imagining that he gave me spiritual comfort – although in a sense, without knowing it, I suppose that's just what he did . . . I was on holiday in Athens, walking very late at night in a definitely insalubrious area of town, not the kind of place where tourists usually go – and there's no need whatsoever to ask what I was doing there – anyway, I was hoping to find a cruising taxi to get me back to my hotel, felt like having a little *wash* to tell you the truth, but what came cruising was a bishop.' Felix chuckled at the memory.

'And?'

'Nothing. I wasn't interested and they drove off to look elsewhere. Because that was the whole point you see, Tasos, the bishop wasn't alone, he had his driver with him . . . I don't say that English bishops or any other bishops might not go out kerb-crawling from time to time, they're only human after all aren't they, but they'd do it *furtively*, they'd never ever do it wearing their full episcopal robes, in their official car with their chauffeur at the wheel – think how much money the man could make selling *that* story to the press – and I sort of instantly liked the brazenness of it. I never worked out if they were planning to share me or take turns or something, or if the driver was merely a trusty servant helping his master find what he needed, but I thought to myself, "*What* a civilised country." That's all.'

'But Felix . . . presumably you didn't speak Greek in those days, are you certain you didn't mistake their intentions?'

'Some intentions are utterly unmistakable, dear Tasos, and language has nothing at all to do with it. Actions speak louder than words. But you see the bishop apparently felt no qualms about either words or actions in the presence of his driver – and that freedom was what seemed so blessed and marvellous and heaven-sent after the dreadful, enveloping, repressive middle-class silence that I grew up in.'

'I always thought of you as being conceived under a talking star.'

'Christ, no, nothing is ever talked about in my family. I'm sure I was conceived in the most well-bred of silences. Assisi was where it happened according to my mother, improbable though it may appear.' Unaccountably Felix suddenly blushed. 'Anyway, amazing it happened at all but it can't possibly have been by starlight, Tasos, more likely a brief encounter in the missionary position with the curtains drawn and the lights turned off. And all in total teetotal silence, oh God, silence, silence everywhere in fact nor any drop to drink, no doubt about it.'

Tasos, being himself a rather silent person, sometimes took a little while to digest Felix's utterances before responding to them. Thus it was many hours later that he suddenly said, as they lay in bed in the flickering candlelight of Felix's room, 'I liked your message on the mirror last week.'

'The chattering parrot that was not only forgiven but metamorphosed into a phoenix. Your modification dignified it.'

'I meant the phoenix as myself as a matter of fact. But perhaps it applies to both of us. Your earlier bit of graffiti was really just a rather extreme way of breaking the silence, wasn't it?'

'Yes, a trifle juvenile and desperate, but I suppose that's what it was. I dare say that's what graffiti always are in one way or another. Release from the terrible pressure of not being able to say something. Expression of the desires or convictions that you can't bear to keep quiet about. Words instead of silence. Much better. Though it is *infinitely* more comfortable to say them to another person than to write them on a wall . . .'

XIII

'A GREEK INVOCATION FOR CALLING FOOLS INTO A CIRCLE'

He came and sat on the bed and talked to me as I finished getting dressed.

'It's very noble of you to put on all those clothes and go and be polite.'

It was an extremely hot evening in July; you could almost *hear* the waves of heat reverberating from the melting asphalt of the road, from the weary façades of sun-baked buildings. Not a breath of air. And, indeed, it's such a bore to have to put on a suit and tie on nights like this in order to make polite chit-chat that normally you'd find me concocting preposterous excuses: 'I feel awful about letting you down, but . . . I have to catch a flight to Kazakhstan in half an hour, I've just been bitten by a particularly venomous snake, the hairdresser was on drugs, I'm afraid, and my hair is currently lurid pink.'

'I like to see you looking so respectable and being so conscientious.' He was laughing at me a little.

'I *am* conscientious as far as my work is concerned . . . as for respectability, well, if I looked *too* outré it would scare the knickers off all the parents and they'd start worrying that I wasn't quite the right person to have the care of their precious offspring for several hours each week.'

'Sorry, I didn't mean to offend you.'

'You didn't.' I had been about to put on my favourite tie, then suddenly had a better, not very noble, idea. 'Can I borrow your blue tie?'

'Yes. Why, do you like it?'

'Not terribly, actually, I just feel like wearing it, if that's OK. Sorry, I didn't mean to offend you.'

He laughed. 'You didn't.' He's been a lot more relaxed lately. 'By the way, how are you getting there? Shall I drive you?'

'No, don't bother, but thank you anyway, I'll get a taxi.' (I don't drive.)

It was, of course, utterly uncharacteristic for me to have agreed to be present at this sort of occasion – a fund-raising dinner, an occasion for former pupils to show off to each other, size each other up, eye each other's wives, and then donate more than they had intended to as a result of a touch too much to drink and a general desire to impress. I was intending to go, though, for a reason which incidentally was also the reason why I most certainly didn't want him to drive me (though normally I love sitting in the car beside him: there's a sort of erotic thrill about being driven by Tasos).

I began to feel uneasy.

'Look, I don't think I'll borrow your tie after all, I don't think I want to, sorry.'

He looked at me tolerantly, said nothing.

'Mine goes better really' (liar, liar).

'As you like, . . .' (and he called me by an endearment that

I don't want to repeat because it was private and because Tasos so rarely uses endearments that each one is like a wonderful, secret treasure).

He was sitting there, smiling, calm and relaxed, at ease. Behind him all the saints in heaven stood ranged, unsmiling, ungiving; they said nothing, just gazed at me with their dark, slanting, uncompromising eyes. I quailed, and unease turned to shame. He and they watched as I took off my jacket, unknotted the tie, kicked off my shoes, unzipped my trousers. I picked up the phone, got through to the secretary and started fluent and not too preposterous excuses: 'Eleventh hour . . . really so very sorry . . . the most terrible stomach upset . . . have to spend most of the time in the loo . . . yes, well, I'm sorry . . . that's nice of you, thank you . . .' and so on.

'What was that all about?'

'I'm not going.'

'So I gathered. What happened, what is it?'

'Nothing, I'm just being silly, I simply don't want to go, that's all.'

'But what's the matter?' He looked at me more closely. 'You're not crying, are you?'

'No' (determined effort).

Do you want to know what it was all about? You probably don't but I'll tell you anyway, because confession is supposed to be good for the soul. The reason I had wanted to go was because I knew that bitch his ex-wife would be there – one of the fund-raising harpies – and I wanted to get a look at her. And wearing his not particularly marvellous tie would have been a way of saying to her, 'Your husband likes *me* better than you, it's *me* he fucks, passionately, wildly, dozens of times a night.' (All right, not quite true, but never mind.)

Childish, wasn't it? Anyway, she probably wouldn't even have recognised the tie, boring old blue ties are two a penny really, though for all I know she might have given it to him . . . God knows, I've done enough rather dubious things in my life, but this one would have been worse than childish, it would have been a *cheap* thing to do. I told you I felt ashamed.

The thing is, you see, that I was jealous: I don't terribly enjoy admitting this: jealousy – the really bad tormenting kind – is like a sort of socially unacceptable disease which you'd always prefer to deny having contracted. It's foolish and pointless, as you very well know, yet once it takes over it's like an endless circle from which you can't escape. Even when you think you've got it under control it tends to flare up suddenly, so that you groan out loud as awful images, sometimes of startling crudity, flood your mind *and won't go away*. For some reason I've never been bothered by the thought of the girl that Tasos loved, perhaps because it was all finite and finished, or perhaps – more generously – because I was glad for him that he had once loved someone even if it ended in disaster. But the thought of that sourpuss he was married to was unutterable hell . . . Oh Christ, does this mean what I suddenly think it might mean? A sour, vinegary pussy, a sulphuric acid pussy, all poisonous and corrosive? *How he could, how he ever managed to get it up at all* . . . (I warned you that my thoughts are not always very refined. And as it happens I particularly dislike the use of that word for the female genitalia; apart from anything else, it once used to have special connotations for me that I don't feel like explaining now.)

You will understand that when Tasos asked me what was the matter I couldn't possibly tell him any of this.

One of the rather lovely things about him is the way he always seems to bring out the best side in me; it's as if he provided some kind of standard of worth and value and dignity for me to measure up to – and it isn't painful or forced but effortless and comfortable, as if these things were already within me waiting to emerge. There's no doubt that I also still have some rather murky areas – like being jealous – but I'm sort of hoping that I'll manage to grow out of them. Till I do, though, I couldn't bear for him to despise me.

On hot summer evenings you don't feel like staying at home. So I got dressed again in more comfortable clothes and we wandered out towards the square, to have a drink perhaps or something to eat, then to stroll a bit through the streets, silent and companionable under the starlight. On our way home, much later, when the faintest breath of air was stirring and the merciless sawing of the cicadas in the park had given way to the trilling of crickets, I asked Tasos if he'd mind making a small detour past the tiny church a few blocks from my house. It's set in a humble garden – a couple of cypress trees, myrtle and bay and some rather tired little flower beds frequented by all the cats of the neighbourhood – and is so old that it's now a couple of feet below street level. It's a very calming place, an oasis; I've been coming here on and off for years to light candles to all the saints and archangels who watch over me. I told Tasos this, hoping that he wouldn't laugh. And he didn't laugh; he smiled at me, but in a friendly way, not mocking, and said something very beautiful and moving about angels which I don't want to repeat. As we walked home he added, 'I didn't know you were religious.' 'I'm not really,' I said, 'I'm just superstitious,

it's like a sort of primitive magic, but it makes me feel better.'
Of course at that hour of the night the church was locked, so
if I want to light my candle I'll have to come back in the
morning.

XIV

ΖΟΥΜΕ ΣΑΝ ΧΑΜΕΝΑ ΠΑΙΔΙΑ
ΤΙΣ ΑΝΟΛΟΚΛΗΡΩΤΕΣ ΠΕΡΙΠΕΤΕΙΕΣ ΜΑΣ

LIKE LOST CHILDREN WE LIVE
OUR UNFULFILLED ADVENTURES

Graffiti, Patissia, Athens

When you lie in bed at night sleepless as the clock slowly circles round the hours, when you wake unrefreshed in the morning feeling even more hopeless, when everything seems too much of an effort, too much bother to make yourself some coffee or feed the cat, then you know that you are more than a little depressed. I suppose that most of us have at some point in our lives lived through the utter misery of breaking off a love affair; with hindsight we smile (either tolerantly or nostalgically) at our past selves and then turn our attention back to the demands of the present. *Tout casse, tout lasse, tout passe.* The operative word, of course, is 'break'. For there are love affairs – very happy while they last – that do not so much suffer a fracture as expire from progressive atrophy. This is the painless way (as long as the atrophy is bilateral, of course); indeed, there's quite a good chance that you will remain in sporadic contact, may even end up as friends . . . Broken bones hurt, though, broken hearts too, and the sudden, violent breaking off of love feels more like an amputation than a simple fracture. The phantom limb goes on paining you: the shadowy presence to whom you keep turning as if to share an idea, for whose warmth you reach

91

out during the night, who should be there, who is no longer there. And you know that there is nothing whatever to be done except to grit your teeth and bear it as best you can.

Leonora bore it as best she could. In her case the misery was compounded by the knowledge that, without clearly understanding quite why, she had put an end to the affair herself. 'I panicked,' was the only explanation she could find. (Not until long months later, when it was too late to do anything about it, did it suddenly occur to her, 'I was angry.') To the insistent torment of '*Why, oh why?*' and '*If only . . .*' Leonora added the desolate wail, '*How could I?*'

So during those cold nights Leonora lay alone in bed, feeling as if half of herself had been wrenched away. As it happens, since her lover was married she was used to lying in bed alone at night with only her cat for company – but there's a great difference between lying there happily, knowing that you will be meeting the following afternoon, and lying in hopeless misery. There should be two different verbs really, shouldn't there: one for that light feeling as you stretch out in bed, every single muscle at ease, and one for the heavy discomfort where your body seems to weigh you down . . . Either way, though, in the morning you have to get up. And day follows day, and you have to wash and get dressed and brush your hair, put on make-up maybe (although Leonora rarely did), put on a brave face, go to work . . . You have to think about going to the supermarket, buying food, eating even if you're not really hungry (Leonora lost a lot of weight during the next couple of months; since she was thin to begin with, this made her look more like a starveling stray than ever). And life goes on.

During the weeks that followed that terrible day Leonora's actions indeed had an air of panic. The memory of his expression as she asked him to go was unbearable; she had not yet realised that the more powerfully charged the emotional atmosphere, the more room there is for cruel wounding; she could not understand her rejection of him and was tormented with guilt and anguish at the thought of how old and tired he had suddenly seemed, how hopeless and weary his eyes as he quietly said goodbye and turned to leave. She ran away, quite literally: she moved to another town.

It is not really so very hard to see that what Leonora was running away from was herself. This never works of course, as you may have discovered. The compulsion was so strong, though, that she roused herself from her torpor, made arrangements for her cat to be looked after until she was ready to send for him, packed up her belongings. (Oh the sadness of disposing of the remnants of a love affair: what do you do, for example, with the shells that you once collected – happy, laughing – on a beach together? You cannot bring yourself to do anything as drastic as throwing them away like rubbish; you know you cannot bear to carry them with you; perhaps you bury them in the garden or in some park, sobbing bitterly, or perhaps like Leonora you compromise and bundle them all into a cardboard box, to be stored indefinitely by friends with a spacious attic. Out of sight out of mind, you hope, though even without such mementos the images in your mind remain excruciatingly vivid.)

Well, even if it *is* a flight there's nothing intrinsically wrong in moving to a new place. What happened next in Leonora's life may not seem so easily explicable. I see no need to mince words so I shall state it baldly: she started sleeping around with notable promiscuity and an equally remarkable lack of discrimination. (You don't need to tell me that she took a lot of risks.) Now it is very likely that this is something which you have not done yourself, in which case you can count yourself lucky for you will have been spared first-hand experience of some rather unpleasant types of men. There's the slam, bang, thank you ma'am type, the type who wants you to buy a black suspender belt, fetishistically fixated on some incredibly outdated ideas of female attire (goodness, how long is it since women started wearing tights?) and the very dreadful type who imagines that his prick is God's gift to womankind: this kind are usually quite good-looking, athletic and very fit, horribly vain – they fancy themselves desperately in their smart white tennis shorts – and of course totally insensitive. Most of them share a conviction that they know exactly what women like, and most of them are sadly mistaken (they tend to make you wince as they put their hand in just the wrong place. Oh dear.)

Please do not judge Leonora too harshly, though. I don't need to say that none of her casual encounters brought her very much pleasure. The truth is that although she did not immediately understand it herself, what she was seeking was not so much pleasure as comfort; like a child she longed to be held in someone's arms, to be kissed and caressed and cared for and comforted, but on each occasion the comfort proved illusory, each unfulfilling adventure ending in bleak disenchantment. Nevertheless she continued pursuing the chimera for some time. What finally woke her from this nightmare, one afternoon as she lay in the arms of a particularly disagreeable man, was a sudden flood of violent, murderous anger. Had she had a knife under the pillow, Leonora would have stabbed him again and again, had she had a gun on the bedside table she would have fired repeatedly pointblank: as it was, she trembled with rage and hatred – he, poor fool, imagined that it was with pleasure – and as soon as possible got dressed and walked out, still shaking slightly. And when she got home it was only to find her cat lying crumpled in the gutter, hit by a passing car, his once glossy black fur matt with the dullness of death. Of course cats get run over all the time, but to Leonora it seemed like a punishment rather than a coincidence; she buried him with the help of a neighbour, then went and lay on her bed in the twilight and wept inconsolably.

After this, Leonora avoided men for a long time. Her evenings were lonely. She tended to go to bed early. Occasionally she ventured out to the cinema by herself, yet on the whole when she got home from work she would sit and read or merely sit and think. Now it was that she began to recognise how angry she had been with Tasos, though quite why she did not know: perhaps it was that his vacillation, his guilt, his anguish – and indeed latterly his impotence – had seemed like insults to her. Or perhaps it was simply that he was not being what she wanted him to be, was not acting in accordance with her expectations, and she was caught unprepared to make the transition from being the protected to being the protector. 'I caused him such pain,' thought Leonora, and 'I was stupid, so stupid, so monstrously selfish. I failed him . . .'

There is never any going back, though. And if you can't go back you have to steel yourself to go onwards. A few days after thinking these things Leonora went out and had her long thick auburn hair cut off. This, she recognised herself, was a sort of symbolic action, a way of putting the past behind her, an entry at last into a new phase of life. Without her weight of hair she felt lighter and stronger – a sort of reversal of Samson's case. It was at this time, too, that she acquired another cat; on her way home one evening she found a starving kitten, a little scrap of skin and bone and dirty orange fur, trying to scavenge what he could from a dustbin. He was wary and spat at her when she stretched out her hand, but once she finally managed to persuade him to allow her to stroke his meagre body he purred out loud. She named him Alexander, then, since this seemed rather too grand for him, shortened it to Alekos. And afterwards, such is the human tendency to see patterns and meanings in the most disparate events, she always wondered if it was somehow magically because of this cat that three weeks later she met another Alexander, also sometimes known as Alekos.

XV

'FOR WHEN HE TAKES HIS PREY HE PLAYS WITH IT TO GIVE IT A CHANCE ... FOR HE PURRS IN THANKFULNESS WHEN GOD TELLS HIM HE'S A GOOD CAT'

People are like animals really, aren't they, in more ways than one. Territorial animals. I am, anyway. When I come home, push the street door open, run up three flights of stairs (well, sometimes, that is to say: it's my way of keeping fit when I feel energetic) and unlock my own front door, I feel at once that lovely expansive feeling of being in my own space. My flat has always been my nest, my lair from which to sally out each day, my refuge to return to each night (and lick my wounds if need be). It's rather sparsely furnished, which is what I like, and its fine, tall windows make it full of light which is why I decided that I could paint it in rich deep colours. All my piles of books and papers might look disordered to anyone else, but they're not, I know exactly where everything is; I clean the place myself, incidentally, for I couldn't stand having some woman coming in and poking and prying and attempting to impose her own order. I often watch the cats that live in the little park below my windows – I feed them sometimes – and I quite understand the way each one asserts its rights to a particular corner: the striped cat with half an ear missing always emerges from the dry leaves under the orange trees by the wall, for example, while the mangy-looking black one comes out from opposite, the little black-and-white female spends most of her time under a bench, and so on. Like them, I feel so possessive and private about my own territory that on the whole I've always tended to avoid bringing anyone else into it (with a few exceptions, like Deborah in the old days before the long climb got too much for her). I generally meet friends in some bar or café, if it's a lover then I go to his place . . . Or at least this is how things used to be till recently.

Does all this make it sound as if I liked living alone? Well, I did and I didn't, if you know what I mean. I mostly managed OK but I can't pretend that it wasn't lonely sometimes, specially round about three in the morning, the time when everything is quiet; on nights when you can't sleep the silence gets oppressive and you feel that it would be so comforting to have someone even just to talk to. I didn't always live alone, you see, and when it ended one of the most miserable things – quite apart from all the usual pain – was suddenly not having that happy sort of commonplace intimacy that you come so easily to take for granted: the small, everyday exchanges about unimportant things, the companionable silences, the knowledge that if you wake in the night he will be there beside you . . . But I don't want to exaggerate: most nights I sleep perfectly well.

Tasos was only the second person whom I allowed to enter my sanctum. When I think back, it's hard to see quite why I did something so improbable. I could say that I liked him – and it's true, I did like him, as soon as we started talking I felt a sort of *ease*. Or I could say, more brutally, that the night I met him was one of those bad moments: I was feeling rather desperate and couldn't face the thought of going home to loneliness and silence. Or just that I'd had quite a few drinks and was in a risk-taking mood. And the other thing was that he looked so desolate – sort of wrapped in the mantle of stillness that comes of being alone, if that doesn't sound too fanciful . . . Well, whichever way, perhaps heaven had a hand in it.

When I first saw the place where Tasos lived I was a bit shocked. I don't mean that it was anything other than a perfectly respectable little rented apartment, if meanly proportioned, but it was such a dreary place: all right, respectability does tend to be rather dreary, doesn't it, but what I mean is that it wasn't like a place where anybody really belonged. Do you know the sort of dusty atmosphere given by furniture that no one has really wanted or chosen? Objects that are placed there not because anyone ever valued them but merely because they'll do – an ugly sofa and chairs that perhaps were inherited from some great-uncle whom none of the family much cared for, an anonymous bed which is perfectly suitable for some anonymous tenant to pass his squalid little lonely nights on: everything adequate, serviceable, but dreadfully, bleakly impersonal and unloved. Tasos's flat gave me the horrors, actually; it wasn't so much like a proper habitat as like a concrete cage in a third-rate zoo. I didn't like to think of him there.

He seemed a bit like a person who had forgotten what he was worth. It made me feel protective towards him. I know most people would say that what I had embarked on was a sort of courtship, a prolonged flirtation, a pursuit: a feline stalking of a prey worth taking. It really wasn't quite like this, though. OK, if I told you that I never fancied him, that I didn't *ever* have thoughts along the lines of 'What if?' and 'Might he?' and various other more graphic matters, you probably wouldn't believe me (and you'd be quite right not to). But when I tell you that it didn't seem the most important thing, I'm being quite truthful. It really wasn't a flirtation. I liked the man, that was all, it made me sad to see him unhappy.

I think he's worth quite a lot. He has some quality that I can't quite define but that sets him apart from everyone else I've ever come across. To begin with, he always thinks about what he's going to say before he says it – unlike me – so that when he does say something you know that he means it. At first sight you might consider that he's rather ordinary, reasonably nice looking, nothing special: a fairly conventional middle-aged man. He has beautiful hair, the very best kind (thick and straight and very dark, just going silvery), which he wears the tiniest *soupçon* of a fraction longer than what one might expect; he's generally an unassuming person is Tasos, but I imagine he has his little vanities like everyone else and perhaps this is one of them. What I really want to say, I think, is that the special thing about Tasos is that you can't help respecting him. God knows why, that's just the way it is. At the beginning I told Joshua about him, then immediately knew that somehow I shouldn't have, that Tasos is a private person, not the sort that you gossip about. Ah well, we all have moments of weakness, Joshua is an old friend and more discreet than he looks; his verdict was, 'Well, he can't be *quite* as straight as you make out, he's got to be the teeniest-weeniest bit *bent*, dear heart, else he'd hardly be sniffing round you, would he now?' Yet I had sensed that Tasos wasn't the sniffing sort exactly, even if I didn't understand just what it was that he wanted. So quite simply I liked him, respected him, enjoyed his company and told myself not to bother wondering too much.

'Respect' is a good word, isn't it, with a wonderfully

dignified and positive resonance: not like 'respectable' which invariably makes the heart sink, it's so dirge-like. I love words; sometimes I almost feel in a sort of paraesthesic way that they literally have colour: 'respect', for example, is a rich, sober viridian, while 'respectable' is the ghastliest of boring old browns. 'Assimilable' – one of my favourite words which slips and serpents its way into anything – is silver. And another word that I'm particularly fond of, 'catamite', is a pearly-silvery-tabby colour. Yes, yes, I know it's generally held to be a pejorative word, but I think it's beautiful with its feline overtones. I've always liked cats . . .

I'll tell you something that I've never quite managed to bring myself to tell even Tasos. The person I used to live with had a cat, a small female Siamese called Titania. He used to call her 'my little queen', or sometimes 'my fairy queen' (did you know that breeding female cats are called queens? I learnt it then). And in the days when he loved me what he used to call me was 'Puss': a sort of play on my name ('Ah, Felix of the tribe of *felidae*, sharp little claws you've got, *feles felix*, my lucky little sleek and happy cat who purrs when I stroke him'). And I did purr, and I was happy, and I was naive enough and silly enough and wishful thinking enough to imagine it would last for ever. It didn't. He took Titania and he went. And in the days before he left, when he had stopped loving me, he said the most terrible wounding things, he knew what would hurt, he said, 'Stop grovelling, you stink like a queen on heat.' I keep trying to forget it but I've never been able to. One thing about Tasos that I do know (I think I know): he'll never hurt me with cruel words.

Actually, what preoccupied me more at the beginning was not hurting him. I told you I felt protective. Always in the past I've tended to be the dependent one – I'm not specially talking about bed right now where such matters needn't be as clear-cut as all that (and anyway, who does what to whom is not the only criterion), I mean more generally – so it was a very new and strange thing to feel that it was up to me to look after Tasos a bit, to cherish him if you want a good old-fashioned word. Very salutary, too, to do everything differently: to find myself refraining from cornering him instead of manoeuvring to avoid being cornered myself, and of course not to begin as lovers and finish with or without friendship but to have things happen the other way round . . . For it took a long time, but just when I'd almost given up hoping he did come to my bed and what started as a rather desperate little grope ended up surprisingly happily. All cats are grey in the dark, I quickly said to myself in a stern voice. It's not that I undervalue myself, don't think that, just that I felt a trifle uncertain and wary of misinterpreting matters.

This is one of the reasons why for a long time we continued to live separately. It's only recently that he's moved in with me. The lease on his flat expired and the landlord wanted it back; somehow the thought of Tasos searching for another miserable little solitary cage began to bother me more and more, so that one day when he suggested that I go and look at a flat with him I plucked up my courage: 'You could have the other room here if you wanted,' I said, then even more bravely, 'Actually, it would make me happy if you'd like to come and live here.' (It always takes a deep gulp and a determined act of will to lay yourself open to rejection, doesn't it?) Tasos thought for a minute, then laughed. He knows I'm a bit sensitive, though, so he quickly said, 'I'm only laughing at the unpredictable aspects of life. Thank you, Felix, I think I should like to very much.' I've no idea how long he'll want to be here, of course. So far so good. And what he calls the unpredictable aspects of life I rather see as the kind of divine providence for which one ought to be exceedingly thankful.

XVI

. . . ΚΑΤΑΠΨΓΩΝ . . .

THE BOY'S A CATAMITE

Graffiti, Ancient Athens

There are sometimes things that one may consider it better for another person not to know. This decision to keep quiet is usually called discretion or tact. And it's surprisingly rare: most of us if we come across some private piece of information are sooner or later tempted to tell it to at least one other person (for not all of us are capable of finding the compromise achieved by King Midas's barber). If we are lucky enough to have a partner whom we trust we may tell him or her about it as we lie in bed at night and no great harm is done. If our judgment is faulty and we tell the wrong person, then soon the titbit is passed from mouth to mouth, what was once private becomes thoroughly public and before too long it inevitably reaches the ears of the person we had originally thought to spare.

George, as it happened, was a man of exemplary discretion. So much so that his automatic thought, 'Marianna had better not know,' was followed immediately by the recognition that in this case his own wife had better not know either. Not that he didn't trust her, you understand, not that various other secrets had not passed between them in the marital bed, just that he knew she saw Marianna several times a week and he felt that this particular bit of gossip might prove too tempting. Anyway, George had acquired some expertise at compartmentalising certain aspects of his own life; he therefore had no difficulty in filing what he had just discovered about Marianna's ex-husband in an area of his mind marked 'Private'.

'Discovered' is a rather dramatic word which may make you think that George had been through the books and had found Tasos to be siphoning off large sums of money, or that he had unmasked Tasos as a crypto-terrorist, or indeed that he had come across him *in flagrante delicto* of one kind or another. Nothing of this. All that had happened was that, alone in town one summer night a few days before joining his wife by the sea, George had gone to the cinema and had encountered Tasos in the company of a tall young man. Well, so what, you might say, what's wrong with that, people do go to the cinema with their friends. Tasos tranquilly performed the introductions and the three of them chatted for a few minutes, agreed that the film was fairly second-rate but that open-air summer cinemas are so pleasant one can suspend one's critical faculties and be amused by the kind of rubbish which would be intolerable in a serious winter cinema; George, carrying the evidence in his hands, pointed out laughing that in summer cinemas even respectable middle-aged men eat popcorn out of a paper bag and drink beer from the can. They then parted and went their separate ways. Yet as he made his way home George felt that he had discovered something. Perhaps his antennae were particularly sensitive and receptive, or perhaps he had spotted the two before he ran into them at the exit and had noticed how at a particularly frightening moment in the film Felix had instinctively reached out for Tasos's hand; possibly, too, his mind was attuned to the surprising things that respectable middle-aged men are capable of; at any rate, he said to himself, 'So that's what Tasos is doing now . . . Good God, I'd never have expected it.' And then, 'Well, good luck to him. I don't think Marianna needs to learn about this, though.'

Of course not everyone is as discreet as George. It was only a matter of time before someone else observed Tasos and Felix together, drew conclusions, and took great pleasure in passing on the gossip to Nicky, Marianna's best friend. Over coffee one sunny September afternoon Nicky in turn informed Marianna that her ex-husband now had a boyfriend. For Nicky (who was George's wife) considered that Marianna had the right to know. This led to a fairly heated argument between the two spouses later that night; I can certainly see Nicky's point of view, namely that it is patronising to decide on someone else's behalf what they should or should not know, yet generally speaking I'd probably adopt George's policy – his wife scathingly called it the easy way out, but it does seem kinder to all concerned . . .

Rightly or wrongly, however, kindly or unkindly, Marianna was told. For an infinitesimal space of time her mind refused to take this information in. I may as well say straight away that she was appalled. It is one thing to recognise that such people exist – in her own mind Marianna avoided using any name for them – though of course you don't number any among your own acquaintance. It is quite another thing to have to acknowledge that the man with whom you lived for a fair part of your life was perhaps always harbouring such depraved tastes. What makes these thoughts even more terrible is that you can hardly discuss them with anyone for fear of being seen either as pathetically naive or, worse, as insufficiently feminine to have held him firm on the strait and narrow path (at this point Marianna blushed painfully at certain memories which rose unbidden in her mind). You might enjoy reaping a little sympathy from time to time for having had a run-of-the-mill selfish and unfaithful husband, but you really do not want to subject yourself to the humiliation of being pitied for something so very much worse.

Marianna could not say just why having a boyfriend (let's accept this rather unlovely word for the moment) was so much worse than having a girlfriend. George tried to point out that when you are no longer married to someone you have no reason to worry about what he does or doesn't do. This was not well taken though, both women accused him of being obtuse, so he changed tack, tried to minimise Marianna's sense of shock, spoke fluently about ancient Greece, about human nature always being something of a mystery, yet that Old Testament Johnny got it right, nothing new under the sun, and so on and so forth *ad infinitum*. He was wise enough to know that the more you speak of something, the more familiar the idea of it becomes – moreover, the more you are able to attach names to things, the less horrifying they seem; thus he used a lot of words which Marianna was not accustomed to hearing and sent her home that night feeling quite a bit better.

Needless to say, none of this changed Marianna's views on either ancient Greece or Tasos's behaviour. As far as the former was concerned, she persisted in seeing her long distant ancestors through a rosy haze of romance: in her mind the Sacred Band remained a group of tall, noble, clean-limbed golden heroes and it never occurred to her that they might have been short, swarthy, heavy-muscled, hairy, sweaty men, nor did she ever pause to wonder just

what they got up to in their barracks after lights out . . .
She knew little about ancient graffiti or the word used to
characterise so many named and unnamed boys; I prefer to
translate it freely as 'catamite', archaeologists render it into
English rather conservatively as 'lewd' though in fact it is
a fairly specific statement of what these long-dead Greek
youths enjoyed, but I have an idea that Marianna would
have preferred the nineteenth-century lexicon definition
of 'given to unnatural lusts'. And so strong was her sense
of Tasos's association with Felix as unnatural that she began
to find it easiest to think that he might perhaps actually be
deranged.

You will notice that Marianna never wondered about the
feelings involved; indeed, she could not conceive that there
might be any. Feelings that do not fit our view of ourselves
or the world are, after all, awkward things to get a grip
on. Marianna's unquestioned assumption was that Tasos had
sought – and apparently found – nothing but brutal and
impersonal sex of a particularly disgusting variety. (In fact
I think it is likely that Tasos found a more relaxed warmth
with Felix than anything he had known with his wife –
perhaps simply due to the fact that he was hedged in with
far fewer expectations of the way things ought to be. Such
a possibility, however, did not cross Marianna's mind.)

George was quite correct when he told her that human
nature is always somewhat mysterious. But again, perhaps
Nicky too was essentially correct in judging that Marianna
ought to know about Tasos's life. For during the next few
months Marianna finally became able to detach herself from
her former husband, to put him effectively out of her mind
and cease to feel such a sense of failure. That she did this by
deciding that he was clearly mad is neither here nor there.

What mattered was that if Tasos was deranged, then she herself was in no way to blame, in no way responsible, was in fact well rid of him. The last remaining ties of resentment and anger and guilt mysteriously dissolved, leaving Marianna as free as most of us ever are to continue with her life.

XVII

ΘΑΝΑΤΟΣ ΣΤΑ ΠΡΟΒΑΤΑ

DEATH TO ALL SHEEP

Graffiti, Irini, Athens

On the whole the tracks along which people live their lives are of a specified gauge and point in a single direction. 'Going off the rails' takes quite a bit of courage; it frightens those who prefer to continue safe and steady along the fixed route where all the accidents of birth and class and time and place have decided they belong. People who are different are a tiny bit threatening – this we all know. Not surprising then that most of those with whom we come into contact tend to be quite literally fellow travellers, proceeding either along the same rails as us or, at the very least, along parallel ones. Only natural, after all, for us to like people who reinforce our own beliefs, just as we are uncomfortable with those whose standards, values, behaviour are too different. And 'fellowship' gives a warm feeling . . . Never believe anyone who claims he's not racist, by the way: for racism (I'm talking about attitudes, not actions) is the simple recognition of difference. Even non-conformists conform.

It was a conversation with Felix that started me off on this – oh dear, I was about to say 'train of thought'; started me thinking, anyway, about belonging and conforming and herd instincts.

'There's always a certain tension,' he said, 'between belonging and not belonging when you live for many years in a country that is not your own.' Then, 'Actually,' he added, 'after a while the truth is that you no longer belong anywhere, neither fish nor flesh nor good red herring (I do *adore* all those lovely old phrases, don't you?), so that the tension is between your own inner sense of identity and your outer apparent lack of any such thing. Quite a creative tension in fact.'

I said that it helped to be able to think in more than one language.

'Yes,' he answered, 'it does allow a certain freedom, doesn't it?'

This was the first time that I met Felix. It was at one of Fanny's parties. I had got cornered and was desperately trying to make conversation with the rather deaf elderly couple who lived downstairs. For Fanny herself went off the rails so long ago that she pays no heed whatsoever to the sort of social conventions by which like expects to meet like; she assumes that her extraordinarily varied rag-bag of guests will be able to get on with one another, and it usually works. But on this particular occasion I was glad to be rescued. Felix came to my aid, steered me across the room, refilled my glass generously and talked about belonging.

'Now you and I,' he said, 'don't know each other at all, have not got much in common maybe – forgive me, I don't mean to be rude – but we are speaking the same language with a rather similar accent and thus have a transient feeling of – what? Of belonging together? Oh dear, that doesn't sound quite right, does it?'

'I think I know what you mean. Something like shared language as the deepest cultural bond, everyone else being benighted barbarians who can only say bar-bar-bar.'

'Yes. Cultural chauvinists, the ancient Greeks, weren't they? But I suppose a linguistic perception of the herd is at least more flexible, more elastic, encompassing, than an ethnocentric one. Incidentally, thinking of belonging in the herd, I've always felt rather glad that when God comes to separate the sheep from the goats – yes, I had a religious upbringing – I shall be one of the goats. Leave the rest to say baa–baa–baa as it were.'

'Have you noticed something else about expatriates?'

'Oh, please don't use that *dreadful* word.'

'All right, call it whatever you like . . . You lose touch, anyway, with the current everyday bleating. You end up speaking a purer version of the language – unless, that is, you get stuck in a time-warp and go on using outdated slang.'

'Like educated Indians still speaking the language of the Raj? "What's the drill for the day, old chap?" and so on – always amuses me . . . Yes. I teach English as a matter of fact, and I'm always trying to impress on my charges that slang should be avoided like the plague, you never get it quite right in a language that's not your own. Poor dears, though, they're all trying so hard to be what they persist in calling "in", such a desperate desire to identify with a wider adolescent herd, that they don't want to understand what I'm on about.'

'Be fair, you can't blame them for longing to belong to a sort of international subculture.'

'Of course. I know. You could say that I myself belong to a subculture that is fairly international. As you may have gathered.'

He smiled. Then half-turned and glanced across the room to where a quiet-looking man was standing by Fanny's chair.

'I suspect you might be numbered among the goats too, so I hope we'll meet again. But will you excuse me now? Tasos is tired, I think, and we'd probably better be going.'

The next time I saw Fanny she said of herself, '*Déclassée* if not *dépaysée* is a very comfortable state of affairs.' (We were talking about the licence that old age gives one to be eccentric.) Of Felix, when I asked her about him, she said, 'He's one of my very special pets.' And of Tasos, 'Now he's someone who seems to have gone utterly off the rails of his past life – kicked over the traces, yes? Well, that's no mean feat, more power to him. I do hope he's not going to break the boy's heart though.'

Fanny doesn't get out very much these days so from time to time I drop in and visit her. She sits like a large stout spider in the centre of her web, always alert to the faintest vibrations: an intelligent and benign spider. I usually take some little offering to lay in her lap; when I visited her late one December afternoon I brought a bottle of the kind of whisky she has a taste for. She was not alone. Tasos was sitting playing backgammon with her in front of the stove that is her only heating. (He was wearing his coat.) He got up and introduced himself, for Fanny always takes it for granted that her friends know one another and never performs introductions.

'I'm interrupting your game,' I said.

'No, please . . .' said Tasos. 'Oh darling, do bring some glasses before you sit down,' said Fanny, 'and we can *broach* this bottle right away. What does "broach" really mean, by the way, I've often wondered.'

The conversation turned to the obscurities of the English language.

'Heavens, I'm not an expert, Felix could tell you,' I said, remembering our conversation at the party.

'Ah, but he's not here,' replied Fanny, 'he's gone to visit his family for Christmas, poor boy.'

I sipped my whisky, of which, to tell the truth, I'm not terribly fond. Tasos it seemed wasn't either; I noticed that he had poured different sized measures rather like Goldilocks and the three bears: a large amount for Fanny, a normal amount for me and a tiny amount for himself. This made me smile inwardly, for it occurred to me that grave, greying Tasos didn't look very much like a baby bear; moreover (once more Felix's words came to mind), he looked neither like a cheerful goat nor like a bleating sheep – nor indeed at all like a heart-breaker; the animal he most resembled with his deep mild brown eyes was rather a gentle and somewhat anxious cow. I recalled Fanny's verdict and had a fleeting vision of him jumping over the moon, startled at himself yet perfectly serious . . . In the atmosphere hung confessions, confidences: more than just a game of backgammon that I was interrupting perhaps, best have a quick drink and leave them to it, I thought. But the worried eyes caught mine a little hesitantly.

'Felix is being very obscure at the moment,' he said. Then, more confidently, as if he'd come to some decision, 'It worries me, it makes me feel so, umm, inadequate when I don't understand what he's talking about . . . Can you help decipher?' He smiled. 'Fanny was just saying, actually, that you'd be the best person, she was going to ask you.'

'If I can, I'll try.'

He paused. Some kind of telepathy appeared to be at work, for when he spoke he homed in on my thoughts about children's rhymes.

'Seeing his family upsets Felix, he won't talk sense when I telephone him. Well, actually, I rather think he'd been drinking when we spoke yesterday though he always complains that there's never anything stronger than cooking sherry in his parents' house . . .' (Tasos felt he had to explain.) 'He does sometimes drink a bit when he's unhappy. He said Christmas would be a penance, like walking to Jerusalem with dried peas in his shoes – all right, that bit I could understand – then something about his bed being a place of discomfort, not requiring a pea to keep him tossing and turning all night . . . I think he meant "pea" the kind that you eat rather than "pee" the kind that you tend to need in the night when you've been drinking, which is what I first thought he was talking about, because he went on about cold pease porridge for Christmas dinner, "no sixpences in it either, they'll send me to Norwich on a roundabout route to Coventry where I've been for ages anyway," he said, and something about being the man in the moon. I tried to get him to explain, but all he would say was, "Rhymes for miserable children, Tasos." Then off again about sheep erring and straying, about sheep and scapegoats, bleating and bags of wool, saying yes when you didn't dare say no, and being the black sheep in the flock . . . That bit made sense . . . "Fucking Francis and rogering Roger and doing unspeakable things to poor Willy," he said when I asked what he was doing. "Sheepish little Francis, to whose destruction I drink regularly, gets an ovine fuck." I'm sorry,' Tasos suddenly looked embarrassed, 'that wasn't particularly discreet, but I think it all had something to do with the bit that went before. It was hard to know the right thing to say,' he added.

'So what did you say, Tasos?' asked Fanny.

'Oh, I told him just to change his ticket and come straight home, not to stay for Christmas.'

'That was a good thing to say.' Fanny patted his hand: 'Look, I know about Francis. You don't have to worry about Francis, Tasos, and I imagine not about the other two either. Just ask him, darling, and he'll probably tell you.'

Tasos turned to me and enquired with great simplicity:

'Does "rogering" actually mean something, or is it just one of his made-up words?'

'Yes, it means something,' I said, and explained. For good measure I explained "willy" as well, since it seemed to belong in the same context though I had no idea what this context was.

Tasos said nothing for a moment, clearly thinking. Then:

'F.R.W. are Felix's initials.'

'Well then,' Fanny looked at him steadily.

'I don't think I need ask, he'll tell me if he wants to.'

Fanny smiled quietly in approbation. I provided a brief exegesis of the nursery rhyme and fairy story references. 'Miserable children . . . I see . . . oh damn,' was Tasos's only comment, followed by polite and suddenly formal thanks for my help. I judged it was time to leave them, put down my barely tasted glass of whisky with some relief, and made my excuses with equal formality.

As usual when it rains, the traffic was particularly slow that winter evening and it took me a long time to get home. First gear, second gear, inching my way along, windscreen wipers working full blast, cocooned in my warm car in the time-out-of-time that is a traffic jam, I had plenty of opportunity to ponder language and belonging and families and going off the rails of predictable existence. I thought of Fanny, sitting firmly in her chair, arthritic hands on her lap, weaving her subtle webs of affection and support for her motley collection of friends. And I thought of Tasos and Felix – both of whom I had met just once – and wondered to what extent they spoke the same language and were travelling along the same track. Other people's relationships are of course always quite impenetrable (which is why one is invariably curious). Fanny, fiercely protective of Felix, prayed that he would not get badly hurt. Thinking over my first impressions of them both, I considered the idea that in fact Felix might be the tougher of the two, that if it all ended in heartbreak, as Fanny feared, things might happen the other way round, that it might be Tasos who would suffer the crueller wound . . . But of course I hardly knew them. At any rate, I concluded as I finally turned into my own street, there does at least seem to be quite a lot of kindness there.

XVIII

'IT'S VERY ODD THAT SAILOR-MEN
SHOULD TALK SO VERY QUEER –
AND THEN HE HITCH'D HIS TROUSERS
UP, AS IS, I'M TOLD, THEIR USE,
IT'S VERY ODD THAT SAILOR-MEN
SHOULD WEAR THOSE THINGS SO LOOSE'

Tasos's clothes are a bit of a disaster really. The thing is that he just doesn't have much visual sense; he regards clothes as merely something to cover his body with, and as long as they're reasonably appropriate and decent (and warm enough or cool enough as the case may be) he doesn't give them a second thought. I like to feel comfortably warm or cool of course, and I *always* dress appropriately, but there's a lot more to it than that. Quite apart from the delight that colours and textures give, it's a lovely form of self-expression . . . And then one always wants to look one's best, doesn't one? Or so you'd have thought – but Tasos really and truly doesn't seem to care. When I first began to get to know him I itched to take him in hand and do something about it, get him to throw most of his clothes away and come out and buy a few really good things that would suit him (under my guidance). Then I thought, 'Well, the poor man's paying out so much in maintenance to that woman that perhaps he wouldn't feel able to spend a lot of money on clothes right now' (for the things I like tend to be expensive). So I bided my time and said nothing. Just as well really, for later on, after he moved in with me, when I was having a good think about things, I realised that trying to make him dress according to my ideas would have been a dreadfully impertinent interference and – worse – a sort of possessive proclamation (like holding someone's hand aggressively in public): a way of saying, 'He's mine.' And he isn't, of course . . . And equally of course the truth is that I like him just exactly the way he is, clothes and all. So I compromise, occasionally giving him something really nice as a present. For his last birthday I gave him a wonderful cashmere pullover of the palest of pale ash greys, and he looks as marvellous in it as I knew he would. It even does something for his otherwise dreary old grey trousers.

Well, even if I don't do much about Tasos's wardrobe it doesn't mean that I've stopped bothering about my own. I've always loved clothes and I know what looks good on me. There's something else too: I know how to get all the details right so that the total impression that comes across is just precisely what one wants. Not many people can do this, by the way; I've noticed, for instance, that an awful lot of otherwise elegant and well-dressed women tend to *overdo* it – they haven't got the sense of restraint that tells them when to stop. I'll give you an example of what I mean. My hair is that very English colour which is generally known as mouse and my eyes are what someone in a fit of northern romance once called rain-coloured. (After the romance faded it occurred to me that he might have got that out of a book, but never mind.) Anyway, a few years ago I was toying with the idea of going blond, and even considered navy-blue contact lenses; what made me change my mind was that I had just had my black trousers made – the softest and smoothest of black leather and absolutely skin-tight, *figure-hugging* as they coyly say in the advertisements for sexy underwear – and I decided that the combination of such trousers and well-cut mouse hair was subtle, whereas with blond hair it would all have been rather too much, even a tiny bit tarty perhaps. (Dark blue eyes still would have looked good but in the end I couldn't face putting lenses into my eyes: even vanity has its limits.)

Hair, by the way, has to be well cut and utterly clean. I'm always absolutely firm at the hairdressers that I will not have anything whatsoever sprayed on it – for who'd ever want to touch hair that is as stiff as barbed wire and faintly sticky with that dreadful lacquer – quite apart from its nauseating smell? My own is thick and curly, and on the whole I wear it fairly short – which is why I go to the hairdressers so often. Once I did try having it cut differently, a bit longer. Joshua was terribly rude about it, he said, 'Oh, so we're going in for the Little Miss Muffet look now are we, what's it going to be next, darling, Little Lord Fauntleroy?' I wasn't particularly hurt, for I know that when his teasing turns into cheap bitchery it usually means he's unhappy, but in the end I thought he perhaps had a point so I now keep it shortish.

But I didn't really mean to get side-tracked about hair, for what I was thinking of was my black trousers. I generally used to wear them with my Hamlet shirt, not silk – too banal – but the very finest cotton lawn. And they're exquisite, my black trousers, they're really beautiful though I say it myself; good for my morale, too, knowing that everyone would look up (one way of putting it) when I walked into the room wearing them. I take a lot of care of all my clothes but I've always taken special care of these trousers. Now, if you have a really favourite pair of shoes you polish them regularly, don't you, to keep the leather supple and uncreased. Well I polish my trousers; don't imagine that I use any ordinary old common or garden black shoe polish, though – I have a special colourless cream for them that I get in Rome. And polishing trousers is rather like shrinking jeans in the bath, in that you have to be wearing them to do it properly. I *can* do it by myself but I must admit it's rather nice to have some help. Over the years, apart from one all-too-brief hiatus, Joshua has been my main polisher . . .

I've known Joshua for ages, since I was at university: when I was an undergraduate he was a postgraduate with some minor teaching responsibilities and was supposed one term to be supervising me. As it happens, most of our supervisions took place in bed – and I'm quite sure I learnt a lot more about English literature on Joshua's rather hard and lumpy mattress than I would ever have done in the library. He would expect me every week to produce the worst line of English poetry that I could come up with. My first effort – Simon Lee's poor old swollen ankles – went down quite well ('mm, delectable little ankles *you've* got, sweet boy, but that's not the bit we want swelling, is it now?'). I later scored quite high with 'Tirra lirra by the river sang Sir Lancelot' (can't you just imagine him prancing along with his pointy shoes?), but I got a special prize for the couplet 'Where seeing a naked man, she screech'd for fear (Such sights as this to tender maids are rare)', though half an hour or so later as he reached for his cigarettes he reminded me that anyone with the guts to pronounce, 'All they that love not boys and tobacco be fools' at a time when smoking was probably almost as *mal vu* as it is today and sodomy a capital offence could be forgiven any amount of bad verse . . . Ah well, that was a long time ago. But we both ended up living here; Joshua, incidentally, still smokes too much and says one of the things he likes about this country is that everyone smokes so he's not a pariah. And we've gone on having various pleasant little interludes from time to time. The trouser sessions always appealed to his fantasy (if truth be told, I've sometimes suspected that Joshua has just the faintest tinge of sadism in his make-up): for the thing is that when your trousers are being polished you can neither sit nor lie down for fear of the cream drying unevenly in creases, you have to remain standing, and of course until it does dry and you've rubbed them all over with a soft cloth you can't possibly, *under any circumstances*, take them off. Well, I dare say you can imagine – among other things, terrible fits of giggles because I'm ticklish.

I suppose I'm rambling on a bit. The reason is that I've been thinking of a lot of things recently and among my other thoughts was the recognition that I haven't worn my black trousers for quite a long time. I haven't, in fact, really been out by myself in the evening for quite some time – for of course they were always evening trousers, don't imagine I'd ever wear anything like that for work . . . Naturally I still put them on from time to time to look after them and also to check that I'm not getting fat; the first check is whether I can still zip them up and the second whether I can still sit down in them. So far I can. The thing is, though, that they are not really Tasos-type clothes. He has never ever said a word about anything that I wear (I like to think that this is due to his native tact and tolerance rather than that he simply hasn't noticed), but it has occurred to me that I've been getting just the faintest bit more conservative, more *sober*, in my sartorial self-expression. The last time I was in London I sat opposite a good-looking young couple in the train, one of them with well-kept ultramarine blue hair, both wearing sailor trousers;

I liked the look of them and thought to myself that I might get a pair for the summer, close fitting over the hips then looser, folded in those wonderful horizontal creases, and of course with that amazing buttoned placket in front instead of ordinary flies with a zip . . . Naturally I had assumed that the couple were both boys, then as the blue-haired one got up to leave I suddenly saw that she was a girl and that her companion really *was* a sailor. It just goes to show that you shouldn't jump to conclusions. I decided there and then against sailor trousers for myself.

You see, even if Tasos himself doesn't mind what I wear, I wouldn't want to embarrass him if we ran into any of his acquaintances, like we did once last summer at the cinema (luckily that evening I was elegant and muted in shades of cream and beige). Also one should pay attention to various old adages, *mutton dressed as lamb* for example is worth remembering – and I'm going to be 35 next month. And, dare I say it, I have a little suspicion beginning in my mind that as one gets more confident one needs less and less to impress people; cross your fingers and touch wood, this seems to be happening to me.

Actually I've left the real truth about the black trousers till last. On the night that I met Tasos for the first time I had been going to put them on, then – for some reason that I forget – didn't. And I can't help feeling that if I *had* been wearing them I might not have met him. So you see, for the moment, although they really are beautiful, I think they can remain hanging in the cupboard. If I wasn't afraid of tempting providence I'd say '*Requiescant in pace*'.

XIX

ΚΑΘΩΣ ΠΡΟΣΠΕΡΝΑΣ ΕΞΑΚΟΛΟΥΘΩ ΝΑ ΣΟΥ
ΦΩΝΑΖΩ ΣΕ ΝΟΙΑΖΟΜΑΙ

AS YOU OVERTAKE I KEEP ON
CALLING I CARE FOR YOU

Graffiti, Iraklion, Crete

I suppose the truth is that people do tend to travel along their tracks at different speeds – which leads of course to a fair amount of overtaking, some dramatic injuries, various chronic aches and not a few divorces. When you come to think of it, the whole idea of living with another person involves a set of rather major assumptions about codes of procedure and speed limits. (As Felix once pronounced – though not in Tasos's hearing – 'Marriage is rather an endless one-way street, isn't it?' 'Yes,' Fanny had replied, 'but there are usually a few junctions here and there, you know, darling.') So what happens if one partner is determined to turn left rapidly while the other is slowly and obstinately signalling right? A parting of the ways, no doubt. And unfortunately the fact remains that there are few simple or painless partings; apart from anything else, old habits of familiarity die hard, some strange residual vestiges of the patterns developed over the years often live on long after the death of anything that could be called love, with the result that the new partner – if new partner there be – necessarily takes on some rather odd extra baggage. The shadowy ghost-like presence of that former person may

124

sometimes make itself felt on and off for an amazingly long time. A certain degree of tact helps here.

Perhaps it is thus not so surprising that Tasos was for a long time markedly reticent about his marriage. Felix, beset by a very natural curiosity (as well as by various jealousies of which he was ashamed and an occasional fairly human longing to hear some wholesale condemnation of Tasos's former wife), made superhuman efforts to be tactful at the beginning and to heed the stern voices that warned him not to probe; nevertheless, he made careful note of whatever fragments of information Tasos let fall. Thus:

'They say the owl was a baker's daughter,' Felix murmured one Sunday morning as he made the coffee.

'What on earth are you talking about?'

'Nothing, it's a quotation, one of my favourites.'

'But what does it mean?'

'I haven't a clue. That's why I like it.' (Something to do with sex, I rather imagine.)

And then about ten minutes later – for he tended to think about things and respond rather slowly – Tasos suddenly offered, 'My wife was a baker's daughter.' (Felix noted the past tense.) 'More or less, anyway – her father owned a rather grand patisserie.'

'Is that why you don't like cakes and pastries?' (Too much cloying sweetness over too long a period of time? Perhaps not vinegar after all?)

'No, of course it's not.' (What an absurd idea.)

'Well, in any case, much better for your figure.' And Felix, who had an unexpectedly levantine sweet tooth and rationed himself severely, dropped the subject. (For a while after this conversation, however, the owl quotation stopped being such a favourite. 'Oh God, your only jig-maker,' was what he more often muttered to himself for the next couple of months.)

If Tasos tended to be reticent, it was for a rather complex tangle of reasons. To some extent, of course, his reluctance to speak very much of his life with Marianna was simply due to the general difficulty he had with talking about feelings. Part of it had to do with that very natural kind of quivering, vulnerable pride which makes us not want to confess our most abject defeats: this was something that Felix sensed and, as it happens, understood well. Then there is the fact that to admit our partner was a lot less than perfect seems to reflect badly on our own judgment. And to be fair to Tasos, I think we must accept that there was also some perverse element of loyalty, some tattered remnant of a feeling that it is not right or decent to criticise one's spouse – one's ex-spouse – to another person, even if that other person is Felix (although of course this does not mean that Tasos himself did not privately blame his wife for a great many things). Needless to say, various kinds of guilt were also involved. Tasos was half-consciously aware that as his life overtook Marianna's and he pulled away she had been trying desperately to call, 'I still care.' This gave rise to a never quite acknowledged guilt – or perhaps uneasiness is a better word – which remained for a long time like an irksome piece of grit lurking somewhere in the back of his mind. There's no doubt that to be cared about by someone whom you are beginning to realise you rather dislike and fear is at the very least awkward and uncomfortable. (Incidentally, there's equally not much doubt that Marianna's feelings were as tangled as Tasos's – yet her misery at the thought of losing him was perfectly genuine, so that I don't really think it matters the slightest bit what particular brew of guilt and shame and dread went into the composition of her caring.) But just as a sliver of broken glass or some other foreign object that remains in a wound is somehow dealt with by the organism and passed slowly through the body until it can emerge painlessly, so this particular speck of grit was gradually encompassed and contained by Tasos's increasing happiness. Nevertheless, when some years later he learned of Marianna's plans to remarry his sense of relief, of a discomfort removed, was very great. He told Felix about it, but his blessedly guilt-assuaging wish, 'I hope she'll be happier with him than she was with me,' received no response beyond a rather curious smile.

During the early days of their friendship, however, it was of Leonora that Tasos felt a greater need to speak. All the same, he omitted to say very much about the end of the affair until quite a bit later; when he did finally manage to describe his total and humiliating impotence, Felix simply put his arms around him, and after a while said thoughtfully, 'I don't think it was your wife who did it, Tasos, you did it to yourself.' Then, 'Never mind, love, confessing the things that really hurt always makes one feel *infinitely* better about them.' And after another pause, in lighter mode, 'A propos, in the old days before I met Deborah I was actually wondering whether I hadn't better convert to Catholicism in order to have someone to confess to. It did seem a trifle *extreme* though.' By this time Tasos and Felix were beginning to arrive at some sort of understanding of one another, yet this declaration left Tasos unsure of how seriously it was meant.

During another of these conversations, as they sat on the balcony late at night looking out over the darkness of the little park, Tasos reported Leonora's declaration that any man who claimed his wife did not understand him would be kicked out of her bed and out of her life forthwith.

'Oh Tasos, *don't* tell me you ever said anything like that.'

'Of course I didn't' (with a trace of annoyance).

'So did your wife understand you?' Felix couldn't resist asking.

A long pause. Then, 'Either not at all or else too well. I don't know. She did understand how to hurt me, I suppose.'

Felix's turn to be silent for a moment. Then, wryly, 'Oh God, they always do, Tasos, they always do. The other person is invariably *all* too well aware of those desperate little chinks in one's armour.'

(And in parentheses I'm afraid I have to say that Felix was to some extent correct in this pessimistic view. Not much doubt that we are all blindly seeking the kind of love which succours rather than crushes, yet – if you think about it – it does require a certain courage to allow another person to hold you in the palm of his or her hand; you can only trust and hope that he or she will not find out the tender spots or, discovering them, will not crush you. It's probably just as well that on the whole most people take this risk impetuously, without too much thought.)

Be this as it may, the question about which Felix had wondered almost obsessively at the beginning, and which finally he could not refrain from asking, was, 'Why did you marry her in the first place?' Whereupon Tasos managed a slight, tense smile and answered, 'I don't really know. I can't remember.' And added, 'The usual sort of reasons, I suppose,' without specifying what these could have been. In spite of the smile, this is the kind of answer that conveys quite clearly a disinclination to go any further into the matter, so that Felix in turn merely smiled vaguely and picked up his book, and when they next spoke it was on a different subject.

In time, though, Tasos felt able to offer a more detailed account of certain aspects of his marriage, and the strained smile was replaced by a cheerful laugh. They were lying on Felix's bed in the stillness of the summer siesta hour, the shutters closed against the hot, bright light – the kind of burning day when every embrace is accompanied by faint squelching, sucking sounds as sweaty bodies part and come together, when each finally moves away to lie languid on his own side of the bed in search of a cooler patch of sheet.

'You know,' said Tasos in a sudden small flight of imagination (stretched out on his back, relaxed), 'in the village my family came from this is the time of day when ghosts are said to walk abroad – it's not midnight in dark owl-ridden churchyards that is the dangerous time, but pitiless noon out on the silent hillsides under the sun. Much better to be safe inside on one's bed, having a siesta or whatever.'

Felix, who usually pounced on anything he considered to be a euphemism, let this pass.

'Not so many spectres left to haunt you these days though.'

'No, they seem to be more or less at peace now.' And it was at this point that Tasos laughed.

'What are you thinking?'

'Only that *this*,' pointing lazily, 'was the bit of me that my wife really liked least.'

Felix understood perfectly the logic of the apparent non-sequitur.

'Oh dear, a lover of capons rather than a lover of cocks,

my poor Tasos.' Then, firmly, 'I don't think your baker's daughter ever knew *anything* about owls.'

Since Tasos had no means of knowing that Felix had originally seen him as a rare breed of silent, grave owl, he found this non-sequitur somewhat obscure. Too hot for questions and explanations though, so both lay in companionable silence until Felix said drowsily, 'Do you know what is my very favourite quotation of all? And it's not Shakespeare this time, by the way.'

'Tell me.'

'It's "Isn't life a terrible thing, thank God" – and I do *so* agree.'

XX

ΝΕΚΡΕΣ ΟΠΤΑΣΙΕΣ

DEAD VISIONS

Graffiti, Irini, Athens

'What's the worst thing that you've ever done?'

He paused to think.

'You'll laugh if I tell you.'

'No I won't – well, if I did, it wouldn't be unkind laughter, I might smile a bit but I wouldn't mock.'

'I shot an owl.'

She looked at him questioningly. They were in the kitchen, doing the washing up together.

'I had an air gun – oh, I must have been fifteen I suppose, and one summer evening I was out in the twilight and it flew across in front of me, quite low, and I just aimed and shot . . . You've no idea, Leonora, the exultation of hitting something like that, first go . . . It fell to the ground and I ran over to pick it up with a glorious surge of adolescent male pride, but the thing is it wasn't dead, I hadn't killed it cleanly, it was still alive and it died about thirty seconds later in my hands . . . It was a scops owl, Athena's little owl. To tell you the truth,' he added after a moment, 'I never shot anything again. Only targets.'

She came and stood behind him as he bent over the

sink, put her arms around his waist, hugged him briefly. He turned.

'You see, it wasn't just that I killed it, that one minute it was alive and private and complete and the next minute only a pathetic bundle of bloody feathers – it was that there wasn't any *reason* for killing it, nothing but a passing whim. I shot at it because I happened to be there, it happened to be there, it moved, that was all really. And it's precisely because it was so pointless, so *wanton* if you like, that I think it's the worst thing I ever did. What about you?'

'Oh, saying the wrong name in bed.'

'You're blushing.'

'Yes, it was rather embarrassing.'

She busied herself with the cutlery.

'If the worst thing you've ever done was only embarrassing you can count yourself lucky.' He watched her for a few seconds. 'Come on, let's get finished here, you're tired.'

Things have a curious way of cropping up in coincidental pairs or triplets: you read about something one day, for example, then see something very similar the following day, the next week a friend mentions the same thing, and so on. Not particularly surprising, then, that on her way home from work a few days after this conversation Leonora saw a dead owl pinned under the windscreen wipers of the bus she was about to board, spread-eagled (spread-owled) in a sort of parody of crucifixion. She suddenly felt a wave of sickness and sat down hastily on the bench at the bus stop. Her feet seemed a long way away from her head. Well-meaning bystanders fussed around her. ('Are you all right?' 'Yes, I'm fine . . . No, really, thank you, I'm perfectly OK.') You can usually get a grip on yourself by thinking logically, hence: 'Quite why popular superstition attaches such a weight of fear and horror to the owl I've never understood,' thought Leonora, desperately attempting to look rationally at whatever it was that had upset her, 'an innocent and beautiful nocturnal hunter, yet bird of ill omen, eerie ghost bird of darkness and the nether regions, harbinger of death.' A taxi passed at this point and someone hailed it for her.

She got home before Alexander, had a shower, lay down for twenty minutes or so, then started preparing their evening meal. By the time he came in her thoughts were thus on other things; in any case, she felt perfectly recovered and did not mention the owl. Yet later that night as they lay in bed her mind worried at it restlessly, so that in the end she asked:

'Alexander, are you asleep?'

'Mmm, no.' He rolled over and lay on his back. 'Tell me.'

'D'you remember when we were talking about worst things? Well, I lied to you actually.'

'Yes, I know.'

'How?'

'Because of the expression on your face. It's all right, never mind, it doesn't matter.'

'You felt you'd murdered the owl, didn't you, you felt like a murderer. I felt the same way . . . You said embarrassment didn't matter, it doesn't do much damage to anything except one's amour-propre which anyway needs the odd knock to keep it in its place. But I did do damage. The really worst thing I did was hurting someone terribly, dealing a sort of cruel death blow . . .'

'Your married man?'

'Yes.'

'You've never told me his name.'

'Tasos.'

'Tasos . . . What a funny little name.'

'God almighty, Alexander, don't be such a snob.'

She sat up abruptly. After a moment he took her hand. She turned back towards him, accepting the mute apology, still sitting but more relaxed.

'He wasn't little. We loved each other, I think, we failed each other, but the littleness was mine. He had a streak of weakness − not his fault − which somehow scared me. I stopped being patient, I wasn't kind, I wasn't even *friendly*. All those unspeakable things . . . kicking someone when he's down, hitting below the belt, snarling and vicious. I hurt him, that's the very worst thing, to turn and rend him when he should have been able to count on me for comfort, I hurt him and I never got the chance to say "I'm sorry". God knows, saying one's sorry doesn't change anything, doesn't mend anything, it's a rather childish idea, I know − some things just can't be kissed better − but even those impoverished words would have ended it more cleanly. What I did, though, was walk off leaving everything torn and ragged and bleeding. A gentle man reduced to a little mess of blood and feathers in my hand . . .'

It is guilt that haunts, we all know this. It is not the dead that walk in the depth of the night but the unlaid ghosts of our own past selves, visions, regrets and might-have-beens, our failures great and small, the possibilities once offered, refused, who knows through what (inadequacy, cowardice), pinpricks of littleness and scars still tender of all the hurts inflicted, suffered. Of our own making then the perils and dangers of the night; of our own finding, too, the exorcisms and expiations. It's only human though to seek a little help, some formal forgiveness so that we may bid the dead past go to its rest – haltingly at first, then steadily.

Thus Alexander held Leonora's hand and she lay down once more.

'Listen,' he said, 'you may have hurt him but I don't imagine you killed him, it wasn't a mortal blow. He's probably fast asleep in bed with his wife right now.'

'He got divorced.'

'Then for all you know he's probably in bed with someone else. And – (more to the point – you are in bed with someone else and it's time to sleep. Wish him well and let him be.'

'Are you angry?'

'Not the least little bit.'

This treatment worked. Leonora relaxed, curled up and slept close against the warmth of his body.

One Sunday morning some time later as they sat at breakfast the cat Alekos brought in a mangled blackbird.

'Cats will be cats, I suppose,' said Alexander.

'At least it's dead, what I hate is when he brings things in that are still half-alive and you have to wring their necks,' she answered.

'Yes,' he said, 'I know.'

'They have such fragile necks, birds, tiny brittle bones, it makes one wonder how such frail creatures can ever survive, let alone fly.'

'Don't underestimate the innate strength of living things. Look what Alekos has turned into – when I first met you, he was the most miserable starving scrap I'd ever seen.' He smiled. 'You weren't much better actually, the first thing I noticed about you was that vulnerable little hollow in the middle of your collarbone . . . But these days he's as sleek as sleek and you're getting reasonably well-rounded yourself. No, sit down, I'll deal with it.'

He wrapped the remains of the bird in newspaper and put it in the rubbish bin.

'Leonora, I never told you the end of the story. The owl that I shot – I buried it, I took it home and buried it under one of my mother's roses. I felt so awful, I was almost crying . . . Except, of course, I was just at the age when I thought it wasn't manly to cry . . . I couldn't bear to throw it into the bushes without ceremony, so I brought it back and buried it solemnly. I wanted to say "sorry" but that seemed silly, so what I said was "rest in peace".'

XXI

'WHEN I WAS A CHILD, I SPAKE AS
A CHILD, I UNDERSTOOD AS A CHILD,
I THOUGHT AS A CHILD: BUT WHEN
I BECAME A MAN, I PUT AWAY
CHILDISH THINGS'

I Corinthians 13, 11

I travel everywhere by bus (apart from other aspects, I don't think I'd awfully like the *smell* of the underground). In fact my inability to drive, coupled with my insatiable curiosity, was one of the things that helped me learn the language when I first came to live here. For I couldn't bear not to be able to follow all the extraordinary conversations that seem to take place on buses – at the beginning it was utter frustration only to understand tantalising fragments here and there. Sometimes I think that if you had a really serious problem that was bothering you, all you'd have to do would be to say it out loud on a Greek bus and no one would turn a hair, everyone would immediately join in offering you all sorts of advice . . . The thing that's been bothering me lately, though, is something that I'll probably manage to work out for myself sooner or later. As a matter of fact, in a way it all began on a bus.

I'd better explain. Last week on my half-hour bus ride home I and all the other passengers nearby were amused by a skinny old woman of the wrinkled-stockinged, bow-legged variety who kept up a non-stop stream of jokes, comments, opinions, stories of the most awe-inspiring bawdiness: she ought to have been on the stage really, people would have *paid* to listen to her . . . (The only people who didn't seem so amused, a bit uncomfortable in fact, were a couple of tourist compatriots of mine – though presumably they couldn't understand a word – but then English people never say anything on buses if they can help it, and if they absolutely have to talk to their companions they use a strangled kind of whisper.) Being still immersed in the kind of thing that I teach in snippets to classes of not very interested adolescents, my first thought was, 'She's straight out of Dickens.' I had to qualify this though after a few moments: Dickens could never have dared risk such lubricious wit, no, it had to be Shakespeare. Or maybe Aristophanes – perhaps she was the reincarnated priestess of some fertility goddess whose rites required chthonic lewdness. There wasn't anything much wrong with her sharp little black eyes, she ran them over me and then honoured me with a couple of barbed comments (on the lines of what the girls were missing and what a pity she wasn't twenty years younger else she'd take me in hand – yes – and give me a few lessons, etc., etc.); the barbs were not malicious though, so I laughed quite cheerfully and responded in kind. Marvellous creature. I arrived home smiling and ran up the stairs with gusto.

Generally, though, the conversations that I listen to are not quite of this calibre. I'm amazed afresh each time by the extraordinary limitations of adolescent speech; for, apart from their own private patois which is quite inventive, I must admit, and which seems to change from month to month, their conversation appears to consist of two expletives and the funny little name they all call each other (all the boys, that is): you wanker. As I watch them push and shove each other about, jostling testosterone, over-loud laughter,

I sometimes wonder why it is that they only seem able to relate to each other by exchanging such an impoverished insult. But on second thoughts, poor lambs, perhaps it isn't so much a sign of linguistic poverty as of extreme honesty, a fair and accurate description of how they pass their time as they go through the agonies of growing up . . . The truth is that questions of age have been occupying my mind just recently. Not so much chronological age, more the matter of growing up – though if one thinks about it it's a rather disconcerting fact that the difference in age between Tasos and me is not so very much smaller than the difference between me and the spotty-faced boys that I listen to on the bus.

The afternoon that I encountered the wonderful old witch on the bus I got home in such a good mood that I suggested to Tasos we could go out for dinner, down to the sea to eat fish; I said that if he felt like driving I'd invite him. Tasos is a good driver and I trust him (more than I can say for some of the people I know – there've been times when I've really wondered if I was going to get home in one piece). He's very relaxed and confident, sort of masterful, in the way he drives and I like watching his feet moving on the pedals and his rather beautiful hands on the gears. The thing is that when we were about halfway there the car in front of us ran over and killed a dog and didn't even stop. Tasos stopped and got out and checked that the dog really was dead; I should have got out with him but I felt so upset that I just sat in the car and started crying. It's not that I'm specially a dog lover, but it seemed to cast a blot on the whole day – I didn't feel hungry any more and I said to him, 'Why don't we simply turn round and go home and have fish another time?' And the really awful thing is that

Tasos got angry with me. He said, 'For God's sake, Felix, stop being so damn childish for once.' That made me cry even more, and when we got there he parked the car and said, 'Look, either you stop snivelling right now and come and have dinner or you can sit here in the car and I'll go and eat by myself.' And he threw a packet of paper handkerchiefs at me and walked off. It was terribly frightening. In moments of panic I have various little sayings that I repeat to calm myself down. And the other thing is deep breathing. What with the one and the other I managed to stop crying in the end and went and joined him. When he saw me coming he called the waiter and ordered a brandy for me, which I took as a sort of peace offering (specially since he's fearfully abstemious himself), and I found that he'd already been to the kitchen and chosen fish for both of us, which seemed a good sign. It was a miserable meal all the same. We drove home in almost total silence. I said goodnight and went to bed because I couldn't think what else to do.

Our sleeping arrangements don't really concern anyone else, but in fact Tasos doesn't officially sleep in my bed with me. When he came to live here we bought another bed for him and fixed up the other room that I hadn't ever bothered to furnish. I never go to his room, for I think he deserves to have his privacy respected, but he comes to mine whenever he wants to. (And I'm not going to say how often that is because it's *entirely* our business.) Sometimes he stays the whole night, sometimes he doesn't. I like it when he does. On that particular night I didn't imagine that he'd want to come anywhere near me, in fact I was trying to get up enough courage to face the very scary idea that he might be sick of me. But after about an hour he did come.

'Felix, are you awake?'

'Yes.'

'Are you crying?'

'No' (with great ferocity).

He sat down beside me.

'Listen, I'm sorry I was so angry with you. Look, Felix.' Long pause, then in a rush, 'I was upset too, nobody particularly likes seeing a dog killed, that's why I snapped at you, don't you see, but these things happen, it can't be helped, there's no need to get *too* upset . . . If I'd hit it myself I would have felt worse, if it'd been my dog that someone had hit I would have felt terrible, but even then I'd still say it just can't be helped . . .'

'I'm sorry. Oh Tasos I'm sorry, I really didn't mean to cry.'

He reached out and took my hand. His lovely hands are always comforting.

'It's not that I specially mind you crying. But it *is* childish to get into a state and cry for every minor thing. No, I'm not criticising, I'm just trying to tell you. You once recited to me a list of all the awful things that happen to people – well, those are the things to weep over if you like.'

'I know.'

'I know you know.'

I owe a huge candle to whichever saint was merciful enough to let him forgive me. I asked him with a little bit of trepidation if he would stay. I don't usually ask, you understand, since it has always seemed to me better to leave him the freedom to decide for himself without pressure.

'Of course I'll stay,' he said.

So you see, what has been exercising my mind a bit is the question of childishness. I've probably given the impression that I cry all the time: well I don't, not very often. And apart from the odd little weep at the cinema if the film's really sad (but that doesn't count, it's like shutting your eyes if it's frightening), I generally only cry if I'm by myself. Deep inside I don't believe that I'm really any more childish than anyone else, but all the same I know that Tasos has a point; not that he said it, but it's true I sometimes project a childish persona or image or whatever one calls it . . . And the reasons really *are* childish: it's all got something to do with wanting to please and seeking approval, being what people (some people) want you to be or expect you to be. Oh dear, a bad habit, what a trap to fall into. I know this isn't the way to make people love you, indeed I know that you can't make people love you . . . though I do so wish you could. Tasos is far too kind to say, 'Grow up, be your age', but nevertheless I think this is the message. And if I know what's good for me – and I do, I do – then I'd better listen.

XXII

ΟΛΑ ΥΠΟΚΑΤΑΣΤΑΤΑ, ΤΙΠΟΤΕ ΑΛΗΘΙΝΟ

EVERYTHING IS A
SUBSTITUTE, NOTHING GENUINE

Graffiti, Nea Ionia, Athens

There are moods when you wish that there was only one way of looking at things. It's hard enough a lot of the time to accept that there might be two points of view: how much more difficult then to recognise that there are a great many more than two, some of them a little oblique, all of them perhaps containing kernels of validity. For it's all very well to pay lip service to the subtlety and richness of the finer shades of grey, but there are indeed times when all you want is for white to be white and black black, for unshakeable certainties to rule.

'I know,' said Felix when Tasos tried one day to express something of this. 'Things are never as clear-cut as one might wish. It's the child's view, though, isn't it, wanting everything black and white . . .' And added, 'I'm perfectly aware you think I'm a bit childish some of the time, but at least I do know that nothing very much is certain in life.' And on another occasion, in answer to the half-formulated criticism that he spent too much time cogitating about everything, 'Oh, not such a bad idea to confirm that one's own little self exists, don't you think – the only certainty one's got, after all.'

These were often rainy-day conversations: wet Sunday mornings that first spring, for example, spent at the kitchen table with plenty of coffee and the newspapers (Felix always did the crossword first, then turned to the book reviews before finishing up with the news, while Tasos never did crosswords and preferred to start at the first page; thus they shared the paper very successfully). Or later, stormy Saturday afternoons in autumn with the lights turned on early, playing chess or listening to music, Tasos on the sofa, Felix lying on the floor. ('I often lie on the floor, it's good for my back.' 'Do you have problems with your back?' 'No, not at all, but that's probably because I lie on the floor so much.')

A pleasant, unassuming domesticity, as Tasos came to see it. Indeed, wet or dry, there *is* something extremely pleasant about spending weekends in the city when most people have loaded wives, children and mothers-in-law into the car and have set off for a couple of days in the country or, at the very least, Sunday lunch by the sea. ('The weekend is the alibi of the five-day week' proclaims a piece of graffiti on an Athens wall. And the rationale behind these regular weekend expeditions is that you work all week and then deserve an outing, a change of scene, some relaxation . . . But inevitably since everyone else is doing the same you end up spending some very unrelaxed hours in traffic jams; the children start squabbling and whining, your wife is tense, you yourself irritated – all in all, the alibi – if such it is – tends rapidly to wear rather thin and the established Sunday evening *rentrée en ville* to be a stressful affair and a great occasion for family quarrels.) What a relief then to find that there's another view as to how weekends should be spent. Tasos had no children as it happens, and his mother-in-law had died long since; nevertheless, he was familiar with this weekend routine. 'On

Saturdays,' he said, 'I always used to set off with some faint irrepressible hope that somehow a pleasant time would be had, and on Sundays I always used to return a bit hopeless and weary' (silence between the two of them as they approached Athens through the grindingly slow, slow kilometres of the outer suburbs). 'So was it worth it?' asked Felix. 'No, not really, just a matter of habit, I suppose. Fairly dire actually.' (Tasos was unconsciously beginning to adopt some of Felix's vocabulary.) Felix, noting every word said, tried to resist the temptation to apply a wider interpretation.

But there is of course an even more companionable way of spending weekends. And indeed after many months of such kitchen conversations an intense Saturday night arrived followed by a Sunday morning spent in bed, whereupon the conversations became increasingly wide-ranging. ('Perhaps a change of scene was what he really did need,' speculated Felix.) All the same, one or two of the questions hovering in the atmosphere were never directly discussed: the future, for example, was something that both preferred not to think of; and Felix – given by temperament to questioning everything – made himself discipline his thoughts to flow along the lines of the *faute de mieux* interpretation. The substitute. The ersatz. The defensive, cautious view. 'Do you know, Tasos,' he had said one rather satisfactory afternoon, chuckling suddenly as his mind ranged along these avenues, 'in my youth you used to be able to get a particularly revolting kind of ersatz coffee essence, supposedly a substitute for the real thing, called Camp Coffee . . . Always made us giggle . . . Gave one *quite* a different picture of those sober colonial gentlemen who were supposed to enjoy it . . . I used to start imagining them in my history lessons, amazing encounters with virile Pathans on the North West Frontier and so on, *terribly* distracting . . .' (And then, less satisfactorily, had to explain the old, old joke: Tasos accepted the explanation without the ghost of a giggle. Felix said in humble contrition, 'Sorry, I'm just being silly, pay no attention.')

This he confessed to me rather wryly a few years later: 'Oh, the difficulties of not speaking the same language – and I don't just mean the same mother tongue.' For it was much later on that Felix began to tell me about these early conversations, the hesitant expressions of uncertainty, the tentative attempts to reassure as each began to feel his way cautiously towards some understanding of the other. 'You've no idea,' he said, 'just how horribly out of my depth I felt. Actually you probably would have *laughed* at the sight of me at my advanced age – well, no, in my wonderful prime really – having such dreadfully adolescent existential doubts.' I don't think I would have laughed but I must say, had I been present then, I would have been tempted to give Felix a good shake and say, 'For the Lord's sake, stop being so damn *humble.*' But of course, if I had been present it would hardly have been as a witness in the bedroom: we would all have been sitting in Felix's drawing room drinking tea and talking . . .

As indeed we were often to do after I got to know them both better, when I was finally trusted enough to be admitted to what my longtime friend and former teacher Joshua always called 'the Felix fortezza'. Before my first formal visit both Joshua and Fanny stressed how honoured I was to be invited to the apartment: 'He doesn't let down the drawbridge for just *anyone*, darling', and, 'He usually gives rendezvous in that old-fashioned café he's so fond of,' they said, followed by the unanimous advice that I should be sure to make an excuse to visit the bathroom. 'Mind you,' added Joshua, 'it's all getting a bit *gemütlich* these days, the place isn't quite as striking as it used to be. Felix said Tasos was too sober and dignified to sit on the floor – between you and me, I dare say what he really meant was too old, but he'd die rather than say so – anyway, after he moved in they went out and acquired some resplendently middle-class *chairs*.' But the fortresses that people build are not only of the material kind; on second thoughts perhaps Felix didn't deserve a shaking: I have a soft spot for him, I respect his courage, and I imagine that he has as much right to his defences as anyone else . . .

Felix himself reverted to the subject recently during an innocuous little gossip session about someone else over a game of chess. I rather lightly said something about having the courage of one's convictions. He commented, 'Easier said than done.' Then paused. Then, studying the chess board, said, 'To have any convictions at all you have to know – think you know – what's true, what's genuine, don't you? And if you really *don't* know, there's not much you can do except bide your time with due humility until you find out.' He moved his predatory bishop thoughtfully and looked up. 'Do you remember some time ago I told you about cats being grey in the dark? I'm a bit telepathic sometimes and I knew quite well what you were thinking – well, humility is no bad thing, but I can't say that in all this time it hasn't *ever* occurred to me that in the bright light of day the cat's colours show up strong and clear.' He moved his queen. 'The truth is that some people genuinely do like their cats to be of varying colours.' He gave me a serious smile of great sweetness. 'Heavens, I *am* being indiscreet. For God's sake, you won't tell Tasos about this conversation, will you . . . Oh, and checkmate, by the way.'

XXIII

'A TRIUMPH OF HOPE OVER EXPERIENCE'

The rather surprising thing is that Marianna wanted to marry again. It would not be quite accurate to say that in her late forties she was out on the prowl, because this isn't exactly how respectable women of her age set about it – in fact, even 'setting about it' doesn't really describe the situation, since until she met Nestor Marianna was not fully aware of what she sought. Seeking, I think, is the best word . . . And when she was introduced to Nestor, another word, 'husband', suddenly moved to the front of her mind, whereupon she had the grace to feel a little ashamed of herself and blushed like a young girl. If some of Nestor's activities had sometimes involved a rather different kind of search, these at any rate did not take place at blameless cocktail parties. He flirted with Marianna, drew her aside, made her feel that their conversation was somehow intimate – though its subjects were banal – and kissed her hand with old-fashioned gallantry. A sedate courtship had begun.

And Marianna fell in love. (This can happen at any age after all.) I don't mean that she actually *loved* Nestor – indeed, she barely knew him; I mean quite simply that he occupied her thoughts, that she read meanings into everything he said or did, that she spent hours getting ready for their little dinners together, that she looked rosier and prettier, that she felt warm and fulfilled. I'm afraid to say that she once even kissed the card accompanying three dozen roses delivered to her door (as it happened, the flowers had been ordered by phone and the card written by the young and bored florist's assistant in between varnishing her nails and chatting to her boyfriend) . . . Nestor's manners were faultless: he never expected Marianna to make her own way to a restaurant, always called for her, and she, answering the doorbell, felt a sort of fluttering thrill in what she imagined was her heart (actually her stomach). He was a person who *touched* quite a lot, took her arm in the street, let his hand linger on her shoulder after helping her on with her coat, and so on. And at the end of the evening he would bring her home and sometimes, not always, accept her offer of a drink: he would sit beside her on the sofa, take her hand, stroke her cheek, kiss her goodnight chastely and tenderly. His strokings and pattings and caresses never disarranged her clothes, never strayed below her waist, he never visited her bedroom. If it were not for the fact that Marianna was so patently happy I'd be tempted to say 'poor woman' . . . But of course one should never presume to judge other people's preferences, and what to you or me might have seemed a highly unsatisfactory and frustrating state of affairs seemed perfectly right to her.

Most of Marianna's friends, too, were glad for her. I don't say that there wasn't an occasional snide comment; after all, perhaps it's inevitable that a few questions hang in the air when a man reaches the age of sixty without ever having married. George, for example, wondered whether it might not be a case of out of the frying pan into the fire, yet, when his wife asked his opinion, limited himself to an anodyne guarded optimism. And, generally speaking, the majority of people are content to take others at their own valuation if there is no marked indication to the contrary. Nestor had always been extremely discreet about the prowlings of his private life, had taken great care to stop just short of anything that might involve *trouble*. Thus no one knew anything at all to his discredit, even if George's and Nicky's youngest daughter did pronounce that he gave her the creeps ('that old neutered pussy-cat is just *way* over the top'); he appeared to be what he seemed, urbane, impeccable, kindly and distinctly well-to-do; Marianna liked him; what more could one want?

Clearly he liked Marianna too. Gradually each got to know the other a little better, neither felt that there was any need for hurry in their relations. Nestor found her poised, handsome and dignified. He liked her restraint and unassertive intelligence. He approved of the fact that she did not wish to go into any great detail about her former marriage, was glad that she had no children, and – being slightly old-maidish and set in his domestic ways – noted the immaculate order of her home as a great point in her favour. For reasons of his own, in part to do with the very understandable human fear of growing old alone, Nestor had been toying with the idea of marriage for some time before he met Marianna. Perhaps at the very moment when she saw him and could not stop herself thinking 'husband' he was also thinking (though in more interrogative tones) 'wife?'; I am reluctant to believe that this means they were inevitably bound to get married – merely, by some accident of fate, their needs happened to be tending in the same direction.

Oh dear, I almost found myself writing, 'Reader, she

married him' . . . I try to set things down straightforwardly – but somehow I can't help agreeing with Helena that Nestor *is* a little bit too good to be true, so that he seems to invite the language of a past epoch . . . However this may be, though, Marianna did marry him. Their wedding took place in late spring when the wisteria and the orange blossom were scenting the air around the church; both felt that a quiet ceremony suited their maturer years, yet a fair number of their friends were nonetheless present to wish them well. If the truth is to be told, Marianna felt a tiny bit uncertain – flustered even – at the thought of what must follow. The bedroom of their new apartment was equipped with comfortable matching twin beds . . . How lovely, she had thought, to go out and buy whole sets of sheets (necessary since all hers were double ones), to start off again with everything fresh and new . . . The hotel room where they were to spend the first night of their marriage was also twin-bedded . . .

She need not have worried. 'My dear,' said Nestor, kissing her, 'we are neither of us in our first youth, are we?' And what followed was brief but adequate, consisting in fact more of the sort of caresses that Marianna had always been happier with than of too much else. I think that both in their different ways were contented with their lovemaking; both relieved that not too many demands were to be made; both glad finally to settle down to sleep companionably in their separate beds.

For there are marriages and marriages, aren't there, and who is to say what works best for any given couple? Passion, in any case, is notoriously prone to fade away – and arranged marriages have often grown into deep and lasting affection. At first sight this union between Nestor and Marianna might look as if it was not based on very secure foundations, yet I have a suspicion that it is likely to provide both of them with what they want and (as long as Nestor continues to be discreet) will probably last.

XXIV

FAR AWAY IS CLOSE AT HAND
IN IMAGES OF ELSEWHERE

Graffiti, London

Do you remember all your past lovers? Silly question really, I suppose, for it does rather depend on how many lovers you have had, and of course on how important they were for you. You may have had various encounters which – well, it's not that you have *forgotten* them exactly, just that the details have become a bit blurred in your memory so that you can't quite recall the name or the place. Or sometimes the details would make you blush for your youthful indiscretions (oh God, that man you met on a train, for example) so that you'd prefer not to remember too clearly . . . But doubtless some were different. Do you ever think of them?

Leonora always remembered Tasos and often thought of him. If I say that she will go on thinking of him till the end of her life this is no exaggeration, though obviously the quality of her thoughts will subtly change over the years, has indeed already changed. In fact Leonora dreams of Tasos fairly frequently; although when she wakes she can never remember these dreams, she knows they were about him because of the aura of feeling that remains with her, a feeling she calls 'sadness', muted yet pervasive. Something of the same feeling is evoked quite suddenly, without warning, by things as disparate as the golden afternoon light seen through trees in late autumn or the sound of winter waves pulling back over a pebbly beach. Autumn and winter were Tasos time. Leonora has now been living with Alexander for almost six years: Tasos lasted barely six months; yet autumn and winter are seasons somehow indelibly marked for ever. The sadness is no longer a sharp pain, more an elegiac ache. Why? What was so special about Tasos?

To an outsider nothing really. Even Leonora herself can't answer this question. If we say 'she loved him' I don't feel that it gets us much further. For inevitably the question once more arises: why? Quite simply there aren't any explanations. You'd think this was so obvious that it wouldn't need stating, yet to judge by the reactions of Leonora's family and friends when Alexander appeared on the scene one might have imagined that you could love someone because. Because he is better looking than Tasos (very handsome as a matter of fact); because he is fifteen years or so younger; because he shares so many of your interests. And – never overtly stated but perfectly clear to Leonora – because he has a respectable profession, because he has a certain amount of family money behind him . . . To do Leonora justice, these were all reasons why she hesitated for so long before marrying him. She liked him, though. Her family's rather heavy-handed approval was not his fault (her mother irritated her acutely by reminding her on more than one occasion that a bird in the hand is worth two in the bush). In the end she married him in a civil ceremony in the presence of only four friends – two of his, two of hers, sworn to secrecy. When this *fait accompli* was announced in due course to the bemused parents, Leonora's family did not know whether to be more chagrined by the fact that she'd deprived them of church and white dress and orange blossom wreaths, or relieved that at least she'd done it. 'Marriage is not a sacrament, it's a contract,' said Leonora to her mother.

And this indeed is what it was. A fairly happy sort of contract, actually. If Leonora had loved one man and married another she would only have been doing what a great many women with their heads screwed on (and an even larger number of foolish ones) have done before her – yet this is not the way it was, nothing was quite so simple. For Leonora did love Alexander and told him so in the end. Generally speaking, these are words easily said; and Alexander, intelligent, perceptive, was amused by the fact that for her they were clearly a stumbling block that required some effort, though he also knew that she spoke truth. And so far they have been fairly happy together. True, they've had their share of arguments as well as one or two really flaming rows (both of them have tempers), and Alexander has permitted himself a couple of very minor infidelities (about which Leonora knows nothing), but they are both contented enough and feel warmth and solidarity for one another. I think they will probably be quite good parents.

Leonora has told Alexander a little about Tasos and he has listened to her seriously, comforted her sometimes, been kind but firm other times. He's not a bad person, Alexander: a little too conscious of his own good looks, a little too fond of getting his own way, a little too unwilling to accept that he's ever wrong, but by and large a decent, generous-spirited man. He's a realist in fact and knows something that I also know, which is that Leonora is in the end much more likely to be happy with him than she would have been with Tasos; this particular piece of knowledge he keeps entirely to himself. What Leonora keeps to herself is that she thinks of Tasos. She is constantly aware that he is alive, exists, though she does not wish to see him. If she met him she knows she would have to stretch out her hand and touch, touch his hair, his cheek, his hand, his penis perhaps, like some latter-day doubting Thomas, would have to run her finger gently down the little line of black fur from navel to pubis, down the muscular cleft of his backbone from neck to buttock, down his leg from inside thigh to ankle . . . She knows this touch would be an infinitely tender confirmation of something but does not know of what. Leonora knows, at any rate, that she will never speak of any of this.

She will never tell anyone, either, that every moment, every atom of time spent with him was a sacrament. I realise that some people might consider her to be exaggerating; however, the truth is that this sort of feeling is so subjective that it can't be described, can't be communicated, hence 'exaggeration' does not really apply – rather as religious experiences can't be exaggerated. Perhaps you yourself have had an experience – either religious or erotic – of a similar intensity and will thus be able to apprehend something of what she felt. I mean 'erotic' in the widest sense, by the way, I am not merely trying to find a periphrastic way of saying that Tasos was extra specially marvellous in bed. ('Yes, OK . . . Mmm, rather nice . . . Nothing *extraordinary*' might have been an honest description of his sexual prowess, but this sort of cheap scoring – marks out of ten? – is supremely irrelevant to anything that either of them had felt.) Leonora is not stupid and she recognises that in many ways she did not know Tasos, he never left his wife, she never lived with him; she is well aware, too, of some of the things that went wrong, of anger and guilt and dissonance, of inadequacies and cross-purposes. Yet none of this alters her sense of the sacramental.

She tries to remember who once said that the past is another country (Alexander would probably know but she won't ask him), for she cannot help thinking that all memories and images of Tasos have an 'elsewhere' quality. A distant, faraway country. A mysterious oasis hidden among barren hills. A landscape of love, once familiar, now lost, never forgotten. Another world, another self, another existence: gone for ever, yet at the same time constantly present locked in some close corner of her mind. She half knows that the dreams which she cannot quite recall are dreams of a great source of life from which she may never again drink. The sadness thus lives on, though transmuted by the daily currency of her busy, cheerful everyday life into an exile that is not too painful. The memories of that elsewhere land are for ever.

XXV

'I HAVE BEEN A STRANGER
IN A STRANGE LAND'

Exodus 2, 22

Ah, spring is such a heavenly time of year. My visits to that
wonderful wisteria arbour in the National Garden are a sort
of little annual pilgrimage (luckily its flowering often coincides
with my Easter holiday); I love the gnarled old trunks growing
up over the pergola and the scent that so perfectly matches the
colour: a world-weary, decadent, faded, pale chalky mauve
smell, sweetest of sweet. It's a smell that is very conducive
to thought and to communing with angels. When I finally
decided I could risk telling Tasos more about my angels he
listened quite seriously (he never mocks), then said, 'You
know, they're really a part of your own self, their voices are
your own inner voice or conscience or whatever.' (Tasos is
a very *logical* person.) Of course I know this is the rational
view of things – but I do like *not* having to be rational all the
time. So when I close my eyes I see them, shadowy in the
background of my life. They're strict with me, never giving
an inch; occasionally I think they expect more from me than
I can quite manage. Sometimes, though, they smile and offer
me gifts, then watch to see whether I can live up to them.
Several wisteria times have passed since I met Tasos . . .

At first I used to think that Tasos was like some strange,

exotic bird blown off course, gaunt and battered and broken-winged perhaps, landing quite fortuitously in my lap. 'When his flight feathers have regrown,' I said to myself, 'he'll be off.' (If you do decide to attempt nursing some wild creature back to health, you have to be very firm with yourself about not domesticating it.) But he stayed. 'Of course,' I proceeded to be very rational and realistic and reasonable and all those other horrid things beginning with 'r', 'it's in the nature of things that one of these days he'll come across some woman and that will be that.' (I'm not going to tell you what various pathetic little wishful thinking voices said in answer to this thought.) And now, what? Well, I'm rather *humbled* actually, I find that I am still learning my way about this strange landscape suspended somewhere between heaven and earth. Always a mistake to make assumptions about what people will do: terribly hard not to, though. In other words, I have been perfectly aware for a little while now that Tasos has got a woman: I've caught a slightly hesitant look on his face sometimes, as if he wanted to tell me about it yet doesn't quite dare, but in fact there's no need for him to say anything. The thing is, I have an extremely well-developed sense of smell; Tasos is a very *clean* person and no doubt washes thoroughly, yet even if it wasn't perfectly clear to me that he'd been washing with perfumed soap (*not* the kind that we use at home), and even if I couldn't detect beneath its traces the faintest female aura lingering on his skin, I'd probably still be able to register the alteration in his own scent – I licked his armpits the other day to verify this and yes, there was some slight extra green quality, some change in acidity . . . I had assumed that he'd want to leave, that I'd be fearfully jealous, but (I sort of probed a bit, rather like the way one tests a potentially aching tooth with one's tongue) neither of these things seems to be happening. Rather the opposite as a matter of fact.

So I've decided that the best thing is just to leave him to his own devices (nice expression). Anyway, if you really want the truth, fair is fair: on three and a half occasions I have to admit that I've been just the teeniest-weeniest bit unfaithful to Tasos – not very recently and nothing very serious, just what Joshua calls 'a little roll on the carpet'. A figurative expression, not literal: Joshua's carpet actually tends to be rather grubby and unappetising and covered with cigarette ash. But in the old days we used to sit at pavement cafés watching the world, grading passers-by according to how much we fancied them: the sort who didn't do anything at all for you, not the tiniest little stirring – made you wilt in fact – were 'Wiltons', while the sort you went really weak-kneed about we called 'Axminsters'. And the very best of all were 'pure Savonnerie'. Hence 'feeling soapy about someone' or 'acting in a soap opera with someone' or – Joshua camping it up – 'getting all in a dreadful old lather', as well as a whole series of other expressions that I'd better not go into. As Joshua once pointed out in this context, the use of the word 'bagnio' for a brothel is utterly appropriate . . .) All right, I'm digressing and you probably know quite well why: I didn't terribly approve of myself really – though at the same time I had the weirdest feeling that if I could have told Tasos about it he might have understood. I couldn't tell him though, so I can perfectly comprehend if he feels equally hesitant. In the end, anyway, it's probably better to keep silent: we all know the terrible retribution a misjudged confidence can bring, don't we?

Even before the advent of the woman (whom I privately call 'the bint') Tasos was becoming much more cheerful about life. I think the fact that his ghastly wife is remarrying perhaps has something to do with it; apart from anything else, it certainly makes things easier for him financially. It also occurs to me that it may not be coincidence that his wife had to disappear once and for all over the horizon before he could find himself a bint, poor love. I dread to think, no, completely untrue, I'm *fascinated* to speculate just how that marriage will turn out . . . For as it happens I know someone who had some rather scary experiences with the suave and respectable bridegroom. ('If ever you come across him, Felix, just *don't*. Steer clear. Unless you're into serious, and I mean really *serious*, bondage.') Serves that awful woman right . . . But I didn't say anything to Tasos just in case he suddenly felt some vestigial *tendresse* or sense of responsibility or something and got upset, or lest he didn't approve of some of my rather more louche acquaintances.

Anyway, for the time being things seem happy (touch wood) and Tasos is in an expansive mood and actually *laughs* sometimes. Last week we were talking about various things which I won't go into and the conversation turned to all the compromises and *faute de mieux* situations in life; when I said in English (because I've always had a penchant for hackneyed proverbs), 'Well, a bird in the hand is invariably worth two in the bush,' Tasos chuckled and said, 'Yes, quite so, translate that into Greek, Felix, and see what you get.' And indeed it did give a rather sweet little sexy meaning.* (One that I do so agree with actually, although that isn't to say that in my time I haven't had one or two very nice little *rencontres* with birds in bushes beneath the Acropolis.) He's started teasing me a little too, which is something utterly new and which

---

* 'Bird' in Greek also means penis.

if the other old adage is true is definitely happy-making. I was telling him about a rather strange encounter that I had while standing in an endless queue at the central offices of the bank. By common consent all agreed to let an immensely, *desperately* pregnant woman go to the front of the queue; I was admiring her hair from behind – a wonderful, glossy deep chestnut like newly opened conkers – and when she'd finished transacting her business she turned round and caught my eye. For a moment I thought she was going to speak to me, it was almost as if she imagined that she knew me and wanted to say something, but in the end she just gave me a rather curious smile and left. (A slightly gap-toothed smile – isn't it amazing how parents sometimes neglect their offspring's appearance? I'm sure a good orthodontist could have made a difference when she was young.) But the point was her hair: I couldn't imagine myself going grey, I told Tasos, and would have to dye my hair, and what did he think, wouldn't chestnut suit me? Then I suddenly had the awful thought that I might go bald, and how embarrassing a wig would be, what if it slipped off at the wrong moment . . . Tasos had gone a bit quiet but then, very straight-faced, said, 'You know, Felix, I wouldn't worry too much if I were you, for actually women are always supposed to find bald men terribly attractive.' This – quite the *silliest* thing that I've ever heard him say – warmed my heart.

I watch Tasos sleeping sometimes, a beautiful, still, grave, silvery-brown stranger in my bed. I am indeed, I suppose, literally a stranger in his land and I've thought that he in other senses was a chance, strange sojourner in my land. Perhaps, though, people create their own lands where nothing is strange – or then again, perhaps spring fever has gone to my brain and I'm just being plain silly . . .

XXVI

ΜΕΤΑΝΟΕΙΤΕ, ΕΡΧΕΤΑΙ Η ΑΝΟΙΞΗ

REPENT, FOR SPRING IS AT HAND

Graffiti, Kifissia, Athens

People often say that you make new friends less easily after a certain age. I've never quite known what is meant to be the cut-off point: thirty, fifty, somewhere in your forties? And whatever the fatal age may be, are you then doomed to continue on your path towards the grave making do with the friends you already have, like so many easy old garments, worn a bit thin in places from frequent washing yet still comfortable? I suppose that, as always with such trite pronouncements, there's a grain of truth in this pessimistic statement; life has its phases – this we all know – and perhaps when you are plunged deep into making a living and paying the school fees and mortgage there exists less opportunity or inclination to make new friends. It may simply be that you have less energy. Or – and here I was thinking aloud – it could be that the rot sets in with marriage: for friendships that have not been tried and tested sometimes don't easily accommodate all the odd angular points and spikes of a tripartite relationship, the awkward knees and elbows as it were of a stranger in your nice warm bed.

'Oh darling, that's all utter nonsense.' Fanny was tired and wheezing a bit but was quite categorical. 'Age has nothing whatsoever to do with it, nor marriage either.'

'So what does?'

'Being happy.' And with this gnomic statement she fell asleep.

Fanny used to declare, 'The most important thing is actually bothering to listen to what people say.' And it is true that this is something that an awful lot of us are not so very good at. It isn't only that minor preoccupations of body or mind get in the way ('I'm dying for a pee,' or 'I've got terrible pins and needles in my arm,' or 'I must remember to buy some more milk on the way home'), it is also that the things people say tend to launch us along some track of our own; we latch on to a word or a phrase and are immediately off into the world of our own concerns, our attention withdrawn. Inevitable, you might say, it's only human to relate everything to our personal experiences, yet it does rather get in the way of listening. 'Assumptions and presumptions blunt your antennae, darling' – another of Fanny's dicta. It occurs to me that to say Fanny had a talent for friendship is merely another way of saying that she had a talent for listening: to the words spoken and to those that are never quite spoken, to the words that attempt to shore up the fortifications and to those that desperately seek to open a breach in them, to fluency and stammering and glibness, to heavy breathing even . . .

This conversation about making friends turned out to be almost the last one that I had with Fanny. After her death I kept going back in my mind – in the way one does – over the things we had spoken of, trying in some primitive way to will her to live on by recreating in memory her face, her hands, her voice. Fanny's voice remained till the end sweet and pure and surprisingly youthful: if you heard her without seeing her you might very well think you were listening to a nubile woman less than half her age. Not long before she died she had reduced Felix and me to fits of helpless laughter as she recounted the conversations she'd had with a heavy breather over the phone.

' "Young man," I said to him the third time it happened, "I don't know quite how young you are, but surely younger than me. I am seventy-eight years old and not at all a suitable object for your fantasies, so why don't you just talk to me instead?" He did, you know, he rang me several times after that and told me all about himself.'

And Fanny proceeded to describe in salacious detail this not so young man's rather improbable problems and the equally unlikely practical advice she'd given him. (Only Fanny could end up being friendly with a lonely masturbator on the other end of the telephone.) 'It's not kind to laugh,' she said as Felix begged her to stop before he wet himself, 'it isn't funny.'

Tasos missed most of this conversation, coming in just as it reached its end.

'. . . It would be too, too shame-making, I implore you darling Deborah, *don't* make me laugh any more . . .'

Tasos went and kissed Fanny's cheek, shook hands with me, then touched Felix's shoulder lightly. 'What would make you so desperately ashamed?'

'Pissing myself. It's all right, now that you're here to make us all stop being so silly the danger's passed. All the same, I *will* just pay a little visit to your iciest of lavatories, Deb, before we go.' (Fanny lived on an exiguous pension and only ever heated one room: Felix felt the cold.) Felix was by then visiting Fanny almost daily, and whenever he

165

could Tasos would come by with the car to pick him up; spring was late that year and waiting around at cold wet bus stops is always rather miserable.

Whether or not it is easy to make new friends, it is hard to lose old loved ones. I met Tasos and Felix again at Fanny's funeral. Felix had obviously been crying but was now calm, Tasos stood quietly very close to him, their elbows touching. Joshua felt much too upset and tear-sodden to come at all, but had sent an extremely large bunch of rather garish pink roses which evoked something akin to exasperation in Felix: 'Florists' roses never smell of anything at all,' he muttered to me, 'but then Josh never ever did have *any* taste in flowers . . . He once gave me a bunch of carnations, can you imagine how dire, *carnations* . . .' Felix's own offering was a wreath, in size something like those that Greek people hang on their front doors on May Day, carefully and lovingly made from pale mauve trusses of wisteria (purloined, he whispered, from his favourite part of the National Garden) and dark bay leaves. The rain had stopped and a brief tentative shaft of sunlight illuminated Fanny's committal to the earth, then the clouds closed in once more. The ground was damp underfoot. On a nearby recent grave wilting flowers were splashed with mud. A lonely blackbird sang. Funerals at which there are no members of the family present to play host and to organise the serving of baked meats tend to end rather raggedly as friends and acquaintances drift away from the grave in twos and threes; I felt it was a dispiriting and unceremonious end for Fanny, but since I could think of nothing else to say or do was preparing to depart discreetly by myself. Tasos beckoned me, though. 'Come home,' he said, 'we'll have a drink.'

Felix went to take off his sober dark suit and reappeared

wearing his violet-coloured robe. He lit all the candles in the house, Tasos poured generous measures of brandy for the three of us (the fact that he was uncharacteristically drinking spirits the only sign he showed of being upset) and we sat on the floor and listened to Fauré's *Requiem*. None of us spoke very much. Felix lay down and rested his head on Tasos's lap and cried quietly. The candles flickered in the deepening green subaqueous light of a spring day drawing to its close; after a little while I got up silently and left them.

A few days after the funeral Felix phoned, calm and collected, and asked me if I would help. 'I don't want to ask Joshua, it would only upset him, one of us can see to the paperwork if you could just give us a hand with clearing her flat.' I was temporarily without a car so Felix said briskly, 'Right, we'll come and pick you up.' This crisp, decisive, efficient Felix was new to me – his way of coping perhaps, I thought: well, fair enough – though he almost spoilt the effect a second later by adding, 'Tasos is a *terribly* good driver, darling, you can just shut your eyes and lie back and enjoy it.' When the time came, Tasos turned up by himself. I realised immediately that Felix was not with him when I heard the lift – for Felix always says that lifts are the lazy way and never uses them, and when they visit me together Tasos invariably walks up the stairs with him. They walk down the stairs as well, I've noticed. ('It's good for his figure,' explained Felix.) It amused me to think that when not under Felix's critical gaze Tasos apparently felt he could permit himself a little laziness. I had assumed rather automatically that Tasos would be the one to undertake the paperwork, only to reproach myself for insensitivity when Tasos said quite simply, 'I thought Fanny's things would make him very sad. And looking out of the window on to the graveyard too.' Then self-deprecatingly, 'Anyway, actually Felix is much better than I am at dealing with bureaucrats, it must be his very great charm or something, at any rate people fall over their feet trying to help him and he gets everything sorted out in record time.' He added with a surprisingly mordant tone, 'Or perhaps they're just taken in by his little boy lost act,' and laughed cheerfully.

The paucity of Fanny's meagre possessions and the bareness of her flat as we took down the shabby curtains and let in the spring sunlight ought to have been horribly saddening, yet somehow weren't. Perhaps all the ribald jokes and laughter had so permeated the room that they drove out sadness. We worked quite fast.

'You've done this before,' I said to Tasos.

'Yes,' he answered, sitting back for a minute, 'when my mother died. In those days I would have found it shocking for anyone to live like this.' He gestured around. Then paused a moment, groping to find the right words. 'When Felix introduced me to Fanny he said that she was his spiritual mother . . . At first I thought that he ought to look after her more, you know, find her somewhere warmer to live, help her financially, that sort of thing, but he got very annoyed with me, said that wasn't what she wanted and that in any case he did look after her . . . Actually he told me that I didn't understand anything about anything. He was probably right.'

'He did look after her in his own way.'

'I know. He supplied her with whisky and they made each other laugh and he loved her.'

'I know.'

We moved on to the bedroom. Fanny's bedroom had rather startled me by its austerity the first time I saw it; compared to her perpetually untidy living room the adjectives that sprang to mind in this chilly bare and ordered space with its single iron bed and plain white walls were 'Spartan', 'military' – or 'monastic' even, I thought with a sort of prescience as I set about removing the bedclothes. Of the three books under the pillow one was in French and two in Latin: all were devotional. I went and put them with Fanny's chess set which we'd decided Felix should have.

It was some time later that I finally asked Felix about the little seed of anxiety which had been germinating in my mind.

'Was Fanny a Catholic, Felix?'

'She might have been, I don't know. Why? Oh, because of her books you mean.'

'Because we gave her an Orthodox funeral.'

'Darling, you are so *sweet* and conscientious, but you really needn't worry about it. Fanny would never have cared two hoots about who sent her off on the road to heaven or how.' (This was the first time I had ever heard Felix use Fanny's proper name instead of the 'Deborah' that he usually called her.) He was silent for a moment as he remembered. 'She once told me we'd all no doubt discover the kingdom of heaven in God's good time, and meanwhile the best reason to repent was that the sun was shining and spring was here and lovely new leaves all waiting to be turned over, and why didn't I learn just to say no sometimes and while I was about it keep off the booze a bit . . . Talk about the pot calling the kettle black . . . She had her priorities right, though, and that's why she was a happy person – unless it was because she was happy that she got her priorities right, I've never fathomed which way round it works.'

Felix put his arms around me and hugged me fiercely.

'New friends are good,' he said, 'but I'm going to miss her so *dreadfully* much.'

XXVII

'ΑΙΛΙΝΟΝ, ΑΙΛΙΝΟΝ ΕΙΠΕ, ΤΟ Δ'ΕΥ ΝΙΚΑΤΩ'

'CRY WOE, WOE BUT
LET THE GOOD PREVAIL'

At night all the thousand and one petty preoccupations of the day are suspended . . . Long, long ago our distant forebears perhaps sat around their protective fires in the darkness and told stories and jokes, weaving a many-coloured verbal cloth, strong and elastic, with which to contain and make sense of all the major and minor occurrences of daytime life. At night the traveller pauses, writes up his daily journal of perils encountered and marvels seen. In the darkness of the night the seeker may perhaps catch a glimpse of that which eludes him by day. It is often easier to say things in the dark.

That first summer they sat up till late on Felix's minuscule balcony on hot, hot nights, enjoying the freshness and the smell of damp earth and greenness that rose from the park, the swooping bats, the trilling of the crickets, the occasional call of a little owl; then later, as autumn drew in, they sat inside, Tasos on the sofa with a glass of wine perhaps, Felix propped up on cushions on the floor with a glass of whisky, all the lights but one turned off and the moon shining through the curtainless windows . . . ('I can see in the dark,' said Felix, 'but we'll leave one lamp on for you.') Later still, in winter time, they lay warm and safe in Felix's bed. And

171

most of the things that Tasos sooner or later found himself able to tell Felix were thus said at night. Felix, surprisingly for one who talked so much, proved a good listener, never interrupting, never offering trite attempts to minimise or console. Occasionally he would point out a little sternly, 'Nothing is unsayable, you know, Tasos,' and this new idea seemed quite astonishingly comfortable, although there's no doubt that it took Tasos a while to get used to Felix's habit of *thinking* about every little thing, wondering, examining, questioning what it meant. 'In the world I used to inhabit nothing very much was questioned,' Tasos once offered in response to a particularly intricate speculative flight on Felix's part, to which Felix, suddenly serious, answered, 'I know. It doesn't strike me as having been a very happy world though,' and a few minutes later: 'What do you think words are for, if not for thinking in?' 'After all,' Tasos protested, 'one can think of important things but there's no point wasting energy ruminating about trivia.' 'Ah,' replied Felix, 'look after the trivial thoughts, Tasos, and the great ones will look after themselves,' and burst into fits of laughter.

It is indeed true that Tasos's world had not been a happy one for him, yet I am not so sure that it was this steady, unemphatic, conventional world itself that was at fault. After all, countless men and women live out their lives in perfect contentment in the same or very similar worlds without finding much amiss or noticing any very great lacks. If Tasos had lived for so many years with someone to whom he said almost nothing of any importance, I suspect that the reasons lay within himself; there were things that he had once half wanted to say yet somehow never could, until gradually they passed beyond the bounds of the sayable and silence set in. Strange, you might think, how he could have gone on for so long in frozen silence that he actually began to take it for granted, to assume that it was a normal state of affairs. Or perhaps, to be more accurate, a tiny private part of himself always recognised that it was not a proper way to live – but then the creeping paralysis affects the will too so that it was easiest for Tasos to go on doing nothing about it. It is of course also always easiest to blame someone else, and Tasos in the secret recesses of his mind tended to blame his wife for failures that were probably mutual. I could say, 'Well, he was simply married to the wrong person, he should have got divorced long before, with Leonora everything would have been different.' (And perhaps it would, though I am by no means certain: with Leonora in the end he was tongue-tied too, when he needed words there were none, nothing, only a tense and strangled silence.) Or I could say rather brusquely, 'Quite clearly the man never should have been married in the first place.' I always hesitate to make such pronouncements though . . . In any case, as the years passed Tasos's world became progressively chillier and narrower and ever more silent.

Saying what cannot be said, thinking what cannot be thought, doing what cannot be done. The last can only have come from within Tasos himself, yet Felix taught him much about saying and thinking. The ease with which Felix spoke when they first met was striking. 'I was lonely,' he admitted quite simply, as if this was merely one ordinary aspect of life among many, 'I needed a bit of human company' – the sort of thing Tasos could never quite have managed to say but which, when recollected twenty-four hours later, made him wonder for a fleeting moment whether it wasn't just something that he *had* said to himself, whether he hadn't in fact perhaps imagined Felix . . . One hot July night quite a lot later, Felix, blushing faintly, told Tasos about the guardian angels who watched over him. (Since he feared mockery, Felix rarely spoke to anyone about these shadowy spirit presences in his life. He also, incidentally, always hated the fact that he blushed so easily but was quite unable to control it; in summer he worried about it less for he considered that his blushes did not show so much when he was suntanned.) Tasos was touched by this sudden confidence and after a minute said quietly, 'You know, when I first met you I thought that you were a little bit like some sort of angel yourself.' 'Well, but Tasos, angels surely don't pick people up, you must mean Lucifer, the wonderful, incandescent *fallen* angel.' Felix smiled happily at the thought. 'I do admit though, picking you up was rather an *improbable* thing to have done.' To Tasos the words almost seemed to have a literal meaning ('stretching out your hand, picking me up off the floor, setting me upright once more. . .'). Both laughed and felt in relaxed and pleasant accord as they made their way home.

Perhaps it was the strangeness of Felix in Tasos's eyes that had made him think of an angel at the beginning: if he had said 'a visitor from outer space' he would have expressed just as adequately – if less poetically – his sense of stepping into another world as he crossed the threshold of Felix's apartment. He had certainly never seen another flat where the bathroom was half as large again as the drawing room, where there was remarkably little furniture, where every room was painted in dark sombre colours except for that blindingly white bathroom, named – according to a sign on the door – 'Delos'. 'Why Delos?' asked Tasos, and then wondered if this was an insensitive question, if perhaps Felix at his ablutions liked to see himself as Apollo. 'Oh,' answered Felix airily, 'it's because no one is allowed to *give birth* in my bathroom,' without further explanation. His explanation for the two mirrored walls in his bedroom was at first a little defiant – 'It's my tart's boudoir' – though this was followed disarmingly by, 'Actually, all it really means is that I suffer from voyeurism and terminal vanity.' He added, 'The reason I like this room is terribly blush-making, Tasos, it's because I can lie in bed and see the Acropolis.' This mixture of modes made Tasos smile and Felix smiled back cheerfully.

Smiles are a good beginning, no doubt about it. And on such moments of free and spontaneous warmth gradually came to be built something that I can only call intimacy. This is a word that has suffered abuse, so I hasten to add that I do not use it in the sense in which it was once prudishly employed in press reports of sensational divorce cases ('intimacy took place on more than one occasion' – how shocking). Felix and Tasos did not jump straight into bed together as it happens, some months were to elapse before they started making love; when they did so it is certainly true that both enjoyed it, yet here too intimacy developed gradually. For the kind of intimacy of which I speak is not something that can occasionally 'take place', but rather something that can exist or not, that can take root and grow and burgeon or not. And it is of course not limited to the physical – indeed, I rather suspect that true physical intimacy cannot very well exist without its durable, trusting mental counterpart. Trust is probably the operative word.

All this was something to which Tasos had never given much thought. He tended to assume that one is automatically intimate with the person to whom one makes love – though he of all people might have been expected to recognise that

175

this is not necessarily so – and thus for a long time failed to equate his sense of ease in Felix's company with the new experience of steadily growing intimacy. Once more it was a night-time conversation that led him to think about it. Felix said, 'You know, it may sound a bit odd, but kiss-kissing is actually a whole lot more intimate than fucking.' Tasos was by now accustomed to Felix's habit of using his own words for almost everything yet this expression was new to him; he wondered briefly if kiss-kissing meant what he thought – though Felix also had another word for this – or if not, then what *recherché* erotic practice it could be that he'd been too crude ever to have imagined. 'If in doubt, ask,' seemed the most sensible policy. 'Oh, it's only kissing, really,' Felix explained, 'not the everyday sort though, not for everyone, not a wildly passionate clinch or a great pawing slobber, just a special, very gentle, tender sort of *butterfly* kissing on the lips. Like this.' Then, after a little while, 'Mmm, nice . . .' followed almost immediately, as he felt the need to revert hastily to flippancy, by 'Well, well – I did say it wasn't for every tomcat, prick and harry but d'you know, Tasos, as a matter of fact I don't think I've ever kiss-kissed anyone with a moustache before. Such a sweet *brushy* little feeling.' As it happens it wasn't so much the kiss itself that felt intimate to Tasos as the secure and happy confidence that accompanied it. Impossible to live with Felix for any length of time without becoming aware of his complicated protective devices, of his reluctance to expose himself: the greater or lesser fits of flippancy invariably coincided with sudden moments of doubt and insecurity. On this occasion Tasos contented himself with taking Felix's hand between his own two hands and saying 'Hush', and Felix, understanding the message, was reassured.

The blind leading the blind? Perhaps. But then this is probably the nature of all human relations. For who can claim in all honesty to be truly illumined? All the same, with a bit of trust and a bit of courage people manage not too badly to make their stumbling way through the dark. Trust, funnily enough, came easier to Tasos, I believe, than to Felix. These were not things they ever discussed, though when once Tasos said rather slowly, 'I've always been a bit of a coward you know, your courage puts my lack of it to shame,' Felix replied, 'Oh God, Tasos, little do you know, I'm scared more often than not.' Then added, with a smile, 'The bravest thing I ever did, actually, was trying to comfort you when I thought you were miserable, because of course I was terribly afraid you'd flinch in horror, get up and walk out, kick me in my sweet little balls or something.' Nevertheless, Tasos was probably right to see Felix as morally courageous and fairly correct, too, in his estimation of himself (the fact that he was able even to consider such matters indicates a certain degree of self-knowledge acquired gradually over the years of living with Felix, either by some kind of osmosis or perhaps simply as a side effect of feeling much happier).

For Tasos is much happier these days. He is still not very confident or at all good at expressing himself in words; thus, in spite of Felix's dictum that nothing is unsayable, he has not been able to find the way to phrase his wish that if the time should come when he is no longer what Felix wants (and he assumes rather humbly that one day he may suddenly seem too old and boring), then Felix should not agonise about it. 'I would like to repay the great patience and kindness he's shown me by making it easier for him,' thinks Tasos, then chuckles as he recognises that Felix would pounce at once on that word 'repay' and accuse him of being incurably bourgeois. At any rate he knows that this time has not yet come. The other thing that Tasos has recently been trying and failing to find the courage to do is to tell Felix that he has embarked on a fairly undemanding affair with the wife of an acquaintance from the old days. For some rather obscure reason Tasos feels a very strong wish to tell Felix about it, though so far he has never managed to find the right words or the right moment. (And indeed how does one say these things? 'I am sometimes seeing someone else . . .': but no, this wouldn't do for Felix who hates euphemisms unless they make him laugh. 'Prissy words, Tasos,' he would say, 'are you really only just *looking* or do you actually manage to get around to fornicating?') Tasos is afraid of not being able to communicate the insignificance of this affair and thus of hurting Felix. What he would like to say if he could is, 'It doesn't change anything – it's simply what you call "a pleasant little encounter", something that I want just now . . . There's a certain amount of easy affection, yes, but nothing important, no essential involvement.'

You might well consider that as a general rule it's probably better to keep quiet about such matters. In any case I believe that this particular little affair is unlikely to last long. There may of course be others in the future – indeed, it is very possible that both Tasos and Felix will occasionally enjoy brief episodes of what each privately thinks of as infidelity. For the time being, though, I imagine that they will continue to talk to each other in the darkness and go on weaving their common fabric. Each feels without thinking that home is where the other is. Felix slips into his favourite church regularly to light candles for the safety and wellbeing of Tasos; moreover, he has recently reverted to the old magic childhood practice of greeting the new moon: touching the gold chain that he always wears around his neck, he makes a deep, wordless wish for Tasos to be happy. Tasos himself simply borrows one of Felix's phrases and says, 'Inshallah, inshallah, inshallah.'

XXVIII

'IN THE VIOLET-CROWNED CITY,
STAY YOUR STEPS WANDERER . . .'

Everything that happens is anchored in its context of time and place: perhaps, indeed, defined by this context. Each city has its style, its mood, its manner of continuities or disruptions. Beneath the uniform paraphernalia of modern urban life, the interchangeable, nondescript, late-twentieth-century currency of asphalt, glass and concrete – offices, supermarkets, airports – lie echoes and resonances that are as distinct as the different languages spoken in Paris, London, Rome, Athens . . . The past lives on, subtly informing the atmosphere, making each city taste different.

They smell different, too, of course . . . Athens lies encircled by its violet crown of mountains, patiently enduring daily suffocation under a dense cloud of pollution just as it has endured all the conquests, occupations, rises, falls, hopes and hopelessnesses of history. When you walk its pavements you will quite likely be concentrating on weaving your way between the obstacles of parked cars, merchandise displayed, groups of fellow citizens who stop suddenly right in front of you to read the headlines at a kiosk. You may well be hot and tired and thinking only of getting home to peace and quiet and a cool drink. But if you are in a reflective mood (a receptive mood perhaps), you may from time to time catch a whiff of something else behind the exhaust fumes, behind even the aroma of coffee and tobacco, the faint traces of thyme drifting from the mountains, behind the springtime fragrance of orange blossom and wisteria, the summer scents of jasmine and of hot, dry, thirsty earth drinking . . . What you are smelling is the scent of the past, the quirky spiritual redolence emanating from generation upon generation of Athenians: lively intelligence allied to passionate convictions, easygoing amused tolerance hand in hand with fanaticism, stoicism, fatalism, pig-headed courage and endurance. You either like this or you loathe it: there is no halfway ground.

There's a lot of halfway ground in human relations, though . . . Compromises, second bests, muddles and mess and disappointments survived with greater or lesser fortitude: tolerance and kindness if we are lucky, fretfulness and worry otherwise.

Tasos, Marianna, Leonora all took the city that was the backdrop to their lives for granted. Tasos loved it, as it happens, knew it intimately; one of those funny little random *fitnesses* in the way things turn out was the fact that Felix loved it too, albeit in a different way – Tasos thus could take pleasure in showing Felix some of the byways and quiet backwaters, while Felix, better versed in ancient history and possessed of a romantic imagination (which he usually took great pains to hide), was able to make the most mundane corners of the city resonate in new ways for Tasos. No halfway ground this, but rather a small piece of happy common ground.

Women are popularly supposed to be more sensitive to atmospheres than men . . . This sort of supposition is generally nonsense: at any rate Leonora cared little for the city and was glad to have left it, while Marianna never thought twice about it one way or the other. Nestor, indeed, knew some of its byways rather well, though they were not the kind that one shares with one's wife; however, he never felt any particular identification with a sense of *place*, knew similar byways in other cities, had in fact been treating himself to something akin to 'sex tourism' since long before this phrase was coined (he himself used the word 'holiday').

Felix was the wanderer who came from afar to settle beneath the bright temple. In days gone by ne'er-do-wells and black sheep were regularly sent off to distant parts of the Empire and perhaps this explains why in the psyche of some Englishmen the urge still exists to drift southwards, eastwards . . . 'The lure of the levant' was how Felix chose to describe it most of the time, though on one occasion, after returning from a thoroughly unhappy Christmas in England, he had suddenly spoken about greyness and depression and misery and the straitjacket of other people's expectations ('Oh God, Tasos, a mortgage and 2.2 children called Simon and Pauline or something'), and had ended quite simply, 'I ran away as far as I could. I'm glad I did.'

In time and place then these lives touched each other, impinged, clashed, came together or parted, with or without sparks. You don't need to tell me that love is born, consummated or dies, that marriages and divorces are made, adultery committed cheerfully or guiltily, that pain is suffered and inflicted all the time, everywhere: there is no city or village in the world where all this and more has not happened, is not happening right now this minute . . . Universal experiences . . . Yet many of the things that go wrong in life – the minor frictions, the major upheavals – bear a closer relation to the particular, arise from expectations that are never questioned until it is too late; as we sadly pick up the pieces and try to reassemble the fragments, there is little comfort to be had from recognising that, though our pain be universal, all our assumptions are of necessity rooted in the time and place that define us. What happened to Tasos and Marianna and Leonora and Felix could in theory have happened anywhere, yet in fact it was in one very particular city that it all came about, impregnated by that faint age-old scent, watched over beneath the shadow of the Acropolis by calling owls and perhaps by countless witty, mocking, irreverent ghosts.

Let's hope, at least, that these spirits are kindly. It is impossible to foretell the future. I feel, though, that on the whole Marianna and Leonora have both in their different ways embarked upon courses that with luck should prove not unhappy. About Tasos, about Felix, I am less sure. I do not know if it is a good sign or not that neither is quite able to admit that what he feels for the other is love; both come close to it at times, but for some reason the word is taboo, even in the privacy of their own minds. Well, perhaps this doesn't matter. Felix at any rate has half-understood that he has come at last to his city, that the gods have graced his heart and brought him back to his forgotten home. I believe that he and Tasos have probably been rather good for one another. Please keep your fingers crossed for them . . .

In the violet-crowned city, stay your steps wanderer
and look around, go and sit by the bright temple
unblinking, unwandering, receive an unreflected light,
a golden hue of happiness, and think
'I have come at last to my city
and my gods, unknown, known, have graced my heart
and they have brought me back to
my forgotten home.'
Then open your bag, take your golden cup,
secret, unique and priceless. Raise it high
and pour a libation. The earth expects it.
Then bring it to your lips and drink:
it is indeed your first, your purest time.
Enter then, place it on the altar, offer it,
the god will rejoice.
And as you go, go with the setting sun –
in the twilight read your fortune
in the distant smiling stars.
Raise your hand and greet them:
they will guard you and guide your steps
in the nocturnal silence, the empty streets,
the city that awaits your arrival.

Spyros Harbouris

A NOTE ON THE AUTHOR

Born in London, Petrie Harbouri has lived in Greece since 1970. She has worked as a translator of Greek fiction into English and has recently translated *Graffiti* into Greek.